Remembering
Christmas

Remembering Christmas

A NOVEL

DAN WALSH

Revell
a division of Baker Publishing Group
Grand Rapids, Michigan

© 2011 by Dan Walsh

Published by Revell
a division of Baker Publishing Group
P.O. Box 6287, Grand Rapids, MI 49516-6287
www.revellbooks.com

Printed in the United States of America

Library of Congress Cataloging-in-Publication Data
Walsh, Dan, 1957–
    Remembering Christmas : a novel / Dan Walsh.
        p.   cm.
    ISBN 978-0-8007-1979-1 (pbk.)
    1. Christmas stories. I. Title.
    PS3623.A446R46 2011
    813'.6—dc22   2011014076

This book is a work of fiction. Names, characters, places, and incidents are the product of the author's imagination or are used fictitiously.

11   12   13   14   15   16   17   7   6   5   4   3   2   1

To Chuck and Phyllis Hamlin, my in-laws. For almost three-and-a-half decades now you have supplied me with a wealth of family memories. Thanks for your love and care through all these years.

1

The Present

It wasn't there anymore. But he knew that coming here.

He'd driven by this intersection hundreds of times over the years, never paying much attention. But he had to now; it was about to be replaced. He wished he'd taken pictures of it, back in the day. Of course, back then there wasn't any reason to. It would always be there.

He sat on a bench across the street, finishing his fries, eyeing the empty corner lot where it used to be. The Bahia grass was knee deep, a smattering of wildflowers sticking out here and there. No trees—those were long gone. But in his mind, it wasn't hard to imagine St. Luke's still standing there. For over fifty years, its majestic spire was the highest point downtown. He looked up at the empty spot in the sky it used to own, shielded his eyes from the sun. He looked down the street two blocks north. That honor now belonged to a most unworthy successor: a cell tower.

A blinking gray stick.

Every day this week he'd come to this same bench on his lunch hour, to sit and remember. Last Saturday, he'd read that the lot had just been sold. A few months from now he'd be looking at a CVS drugstore. In one sense, it was a good thing. One more sign the downtown area was making a comeback.

The church had been gone for over two decades. The whole building had burned to the ground. A senseless accident. Something about a day laborer storing a pile of rags on some cans of linseed oil. A church committee had voted, and a plan to give the pews a new shine had led to the destruction of this beautiful landmark.

The memories he'd been digging for had all happened ten years before that, in the fall of 1980. A simpler time. Not nearly as hectic and nowhere near the level of distraction. You could count on having whole conversations with people. No cell phones, laptops, netbooks, or iPads. No internet. Just a handful of channels on TV. Only the folks in Arkansas had ever heard of Walmart. And only one cast of *Star Trek* to keep track of.

He looked across the street again, at the space that would have been the rear corner of the church building. The picture in his mind was so strong. He could still see the leaky roof. The old sofa in the back. Hear the cash register bell clanging. And then, of course, the peculiar cast of characters coming in and out.

He looked at his watch. Time to head back to the office. But he wanted to get closer, to strengthen the feeling. He stood, waited for the traffic to clear, and walked across the street. The old sidewalk was still there. And for some reason, they had left the little stairwell all these years. Six uneven steps that led down to the door.

If he closed his eyes, he could see it all so clearly.

The Book Nook.

The place where his life had changed forever.

2

November 1980

JD was getting nervous. It was past Egg McMuffin time. Way past. One thing JD could always count on: Art was never late. A dense fog hovered about the downtown area. A fairly rare occurrence, which only deepened the sense of mystery.

JD was hungry, but, even more than that, he knew soon as he woke up he was going to need the heat from Art's coffee to take the chill out of his bones. He looked over his shoulder to the spot he called home, shrouded in mist. It was right behind the old church, under a fiberglass awning put up last year to keep the rain from pouring into the trash cans. It did that all right but did nothing to ward off the cold night air. He rubbed his lower back, but the pain returned soon as he stopped rubbing. After breakfast, he'd have to make his way over to McAlister's, the last appliance store downtown, see about getting a new carton, some fresh packing material.

JD peeked out from behind the corner of the church, eyeing the stairwell leading down to the Book Nook. The little store occupied the southeast corner of the building, in something like a basement. Folks in Florida didn't have basements, of course. Pick any spot, dig a few feet, and you hit water. The church had been built up on stone pilings back in the early 1900s, allowing for a ground floor underneath.

That's where Art and Leanne had opened up the Book Nook some twelve years ago. But the stairwell was the only thing that mattered to JD, because that was the deal. He'd stopped sleeping in the stairwell and Art brought him an Egg McMuffin every morning. Except Sunday. The Book Nook was closed on Sunday. JD got scrambled eggs and home fries on Sundays at an outreach ministry over on Walker, three blocks away.

Well, come to think of it, he didn't get his Egg McMuffin yesterday, either, but that was to be expected. Thanksgiving Day. All the downtown stores were closed. But you could always count on one or two churches sending folks downtown to serve turkey suppers.

Yesterday JD ate pretty well. Two turkey suppers with all the fixings in the span of four hours. Started to sleep it off just after sundown. Got up just that once before 2:00 a.m. to get a bottle of Jack Daniel's before the liquor store closed.

That's how JD knew something was off, looking at the Book Nook now. The lights were on inside. He could see that plainly through the curtains. And somebody had turned on that garland of Christmas lights around the doorway. They weren't on last night. He'd have seen them when he'd walked right by here after getting that whiskey bottle. The Book Nook had been black as night, the stairwell hidden in shadows.

Why he used to like it so much.

He rummaged through his raincoat pocket, past some rubber bands and paper clips till he felt his new watch. Second hand didn't work, but who counted seconds? And the leather wristband didn't latch, but it worked just fine in his pocket.

8:50 it said, or thereabouts.

He peeked around the corner again. Where was Art with

his breakfast? Store opened at 9:00. This was their routine, going back almost a year now. Art would greet JD with that nice smile he always wore, unlock the front door, and hand him a white paper bag with that delicious sandwich inside. You'd think JD would be sick of eating the same thing every day. But the stupid thing was just that good. Then Art would go inside to make a fresh pot of coffee. JD would wait right here at this same corner till Art came out with a fresh hot cup.

That was also part of the deal. JD never went inside.

Both of them knew JD didn't buy any books. Art said that the way JD looked and some of the things he did scared people away, ones that did buy books. Art said it real nice, with that pleasant face he had, and JD didn't feel bad about it. Art had this way about him; whether saying something negative or positive, it always came out positive. Some of the downtown store owners would just yell at JD if he hung around too long, or threaten to call the cops.

This arrangement wasn't bad at all.

He looked around the corner again. Nothing.

"I think you should go inside," said a deep voice behind him. JD didn't even turn around. He recognized the voice instantly: his friend Taylor.

"I'm not supposed to," JD said. "You know that."

"But something is wrong," said Taylor. "Clearly."

"What if I go in there and he comes in and finds me, and that's it? No more Egg McMuffins."

"That won't happen," said Taylor. "You know he's not like that."

Taylor was right. Art wasn't like that. JD turned and looked up at his friend, who was over six feet tall. "Anyone ever tell you, you look just like that new president? You know, the actor."

"Ronald Reagan," Taylor said.

"That's him," said JD. "'Course, you're way younger."

"You're just changing the subject."

JD turned around and peeked at the stairwell again. He looked up. Beyond the corner, it was like the whole world disappeared. He hated fog. "I just want to give it another minute. He doesn't come then, I'll go check the door."

"Fine," Taylor said. "But I think you're making a mistake." A few seconds later, "You can call me Ronald if you'd like."

JD ignored him. Usually if he did that long enough, Taylor would disappear. Art could never see Taylor, and JD found that strange. But then so many people couldn't see Taylor. Once, when he first started coming around, Taylor was standing right next to him when Art gave him his Egg McMuffin. JD felt bad that Taylor didn't have one, had asked Art for a dollar to go buy him one. Art had just smiled, looked right through Taylor, and said, "Now, JD, you and I both know you're not asking for a dollar to buy another egg sandwich." Strange.

Well, it was time. JD looked at his watch again. Just a few minutes before 9:00. Something had to be wrong. He turned, but Taylor was already gone.

Fog or no fog, JD stepped out from behind the corner and walked along the sidewalk, looking every which way to see if anyone saw him. He was used to the stares. Everyone did the same thing: stared, looked away, stared some more, looked away. Through the mist he saw a few people across the street and the bottom half of a few more down at the intersection, but no one seemed to be heading this way or paying any attention. He headed down the six uneven stairs. Looked through the sheers covering the glass part of the door but couldn't see anything. He wanted to knock but was afraid it would draw attention.

Just turn the knob.

It wasn't Taylor's voice, but it might as well have been. He listened, turned the knob, and the door opened right up. He slipped inside. The store was all lit like it should be, but he saw no one inside. There was the cash register on the short counter off to the left. Even had a miniature Christmas tree on the end. All sparkly. To his right, the four rows of books. In the far right corner was the little paneled office, where Art did his paperwork.

Right beside it, where he made that wonderful coffee.

JD walked down the last two steps, just inside the door. "Hello?" he called. "Anybody here? Art?"

He stepped farther inside. He noticed a black picture frame on the wall hanging to his left, about head high. It was that article Art had showed him a few months ago, the one the newspaper did about the Book Nook. Art said it was in the religion section. He'd clipped it out and his wife Leanne had framed it. There was a picture of the two of them, Art and Leanne, standing behind the counter, smiling.

JD started to read:

To churchgoers all over town and from every evangelical stream, the Book Nook seems more like an enchanted cottage than a bookstore. A harbor from the cares of life. Some call it a little slice of heaven. It is run from the basement of St. Luke's Church downtown. "No matter what condition you may be in," says patron Dorothy Parker, "when you walk down those uneven steps, and duck to avoid the low-hanging doorway, and spend whatever amount of time you need, you'll walk out overwhelmed with a sense that you've encountered the presence of God."

Most, if asked, could not tell you exactly why this is so. But if pressed, they will say it has everything to do with the owners, Art and Leanne Bell. This sweet couple, in equal parts and in their own way, seem to radiate the love of God. It's on their face, in their eyes; it flows from their words. Some say you can even feel it in their touch. To be around them is to experience God's grace.

JD stopped, suddenly aware of where he was and what he was doing. It was now after 9:00. A customer could walk in at any moment. "Hello, Art? You in here?"

No answer.

He looked to the front door, thinking perhaps he should run right out, when he smelled the most wonderful smell. Coffee brewing from the back. Art had to be here. JD walked carefully down the first aisle. Noticed a red and silver garland of tinsel, in loops across the top shelf. Up ahead he saw a light on in the office. He was about to look inside but stopped. He didn't hear anyone, not a sound. He looked down.

Oh no.

There on the floor, sticking out through the doorway, a pair of legs. He recognized the pants and the shoes. "Art?"

No answer. He looked inside.

It was Art, unconscious on the floor.

3

He turned the car on. Instantly, the radio began blaring Johnny Mathis's rendition of "It's Beginning to Look a Lot Like Christmas."

Rick Denton quickly pushed a cassette in to stop the madness. He liked Christmas music as much as the next guy, but, please, did they have to start so early in the year? It was just Thanksgiving yesterday. Now he remembered hearing something on Wednesday, a DJ saying something about playing Christmas music the entire four-day weekend.

A moment later, the soothing music, then the voice of Christopher Cross, filled the car. The song was "Sailing," and Rick was quickly taken away to a much better place.

He started singing along. Had the road to himself, why not? After the tense meeting he'd just had with a client, he needed Christopher Cross way more than Johnny Mathis. He was supposed to be skiing right now, but his client had insisted they meet this morning, get things wrapped up so he could fly home to Pittsburgh. Rick was driving back to the CPA firm in Charlotte where he parked his desk every day. A simple plan from here. File a few things, write down a few notes while his thoughts were fresh. Then hit the slopes at

Sugar Mountain, just a few hours northwest of town. His friends had been there since yesterday afternoon.

The chorus to "Sailing" came back around again.

For the most part, Rick mangled the lyrics but sang like he knew them all, got close here and there. Felt he could just as easily trade out "sailing" for "skiing" and the song would work just as well. He loved doing both.

And he loved the fact that he had plenty of money to do both. He surveyed the insides of his Toyota Celica: leather interior, wood-grained dash, speakers in the front and back. Still had traces of the new car smell. He sat in that leather seat wearing a three-piece suit and the tie he'd taken fifteen minutes this morning to pick out.

How much he'd changed from a decade ago, when he'd fled home for college. Drove a VW van back then, hair halfway down his back, stoned almost every day before noon. He would have despised the man he'd become now. He was officially a sellout, part of the establishment.

Once more, the chorus of "Sailing" returned. He hummed along a few measures, tapped the dashboard, then belted out the end.

He *would* soon be free. Life was better now. Much better.

He turned right, left, stopped at traffic lights, threaded the mindless maze back to the office. Traffic was light the whole way, because everyone else was off. The parking garage formed the first three floors of the high-rise where he worked. It, too, was nearly empty.

He took the elevator to the tenth floor by himself. Then again, he wasn't totally alone. He was joined by the Lennon Sisters singing a spirited rendition of "Winter Wonderland." He stepped out and walked through the lonely halls until he reached the entrance to the firm. *In the meadow we can build a snowman, and pretend that he is Parson Brown.* How was he going to get this song out of his head?

There wasn't even a receptionist at the front desk. He made his way past the open center section, a vast array of cubicles he'd been delivered from last year. *But you can do the job when you're in town.* He heard a few typewriters clicking away somewhere near the middle, a welcome sound. As he turned the corner toward his office, he was surprised to see another human. A young clerk hired to assist a more senior accountant three doors down. She wasn't unattractive, but not his type.

"Hi, Mr. Denton. Surprised to see you here."

"Hello." He'd forgotten her name. "Had one last appointment this morning. Just came in a minute to take care of a few odds and ends. How come you're here?"

"Still under thirty days, so I only got yesterday off. But I don't mind. Getting a lot done with no one around."

He opened his office door and stepped inside.

"Oh, I almost forgot," she said. "Hope you don't mind, but I left a note on your desk. The phone kept ringing every few minutes, so I figured it must be something important. Guess you forgot to turn your answering machine on."

"Thanks." He walked to his desk and set his briefcase down. He lifted a pink phone message from a brass spike, saw it was written at 10:30 a.m. About thirty minutes ago.

Your mother called. Said it was extremely urgent. Something about your father having a stroke and being in the hospital. She left this number, the hospital waiting room.

"Great." Rick had spoken with his mother yesterday on Thanksgiving. It was like pulling teeth. She went on and on about the latest things happening down at their little store, how cute it was with the new Christmas decorations they added. Then she asked him all about the things going on in his life. He never knew what to say or how much. He loved her; she was his mom, but they had nothing in common. And he knew she wouldn't approve of half the things he did if he told her the truth. He didn't go to church. He drank too much and too often, had too many girlfriends, not the right kind.

He sighed, dialed the number.

"Hello?" A woman's voice.

"Hi, my name is Rick Denton. Is this a hospital waiting room?"

"Yes, it is."

"I'm looking for my mother, Leanne Bell. Is she there?"

"I'm not sure. I don't work here, but let me check."

He heard her voice, away from the mouthpiece, asking if anyone named Leanne Bell was there. Then some muffled reply.

"Someone said she's here, but she's in the room by her husband's bed. They don't allow phones back there. I'll go ask the nurse to get her."

"Uh, ma'am. If you don't mind—" He heard a bump. Clearly, she had set the phone down. He waited for what felt like fifteen minutes.

"Hello?"

"Mom?"

"Rick? Is that you?" She started to cry.

"It's me, Mom. I got your message."

"I'm so scared, Rick. I've never seen him like this."

"Mom, just tell me what happened."

She paused. He could hear her trying to catch her breath. "It's your father. They think he had a stroke. I guess it happened sometime this morning, just after he got to the store."

My father . . . "How bad is it?"

"They don't know yet. He isn't responding at all. He's alive. They're saying his vital signs look good. But . . . I can't talk to him, Rick. His eyes won't open. He doesn't even look at me when I talk to him." She started crying again.

Rick knew that his plans to hit the slopes that afternoon had just collapsed. "Okay, Mom, listen." He sighed. "Is anyone with you?"

"I've called some friends from church, but so far I haven't been able to reach anyone."

"Do you want me to come down there?" Of course she would, why even ask?

"I hate to bother you, Rick, but I've never been so scared. I don't know what I'd do if I lost him. And then there's the store—who will run it? The doctor said it could be days before we know anything for sure, maybe longer. That's if he survives." Now she was sobbing.

"Well, I guess I could get down there for the weekend."

"You'll come?"

"Yes. I'm not sure I can get a plane because of the holiday. Probably take me the rest of the day to drive there."

"I'm so sorry to put you through this," she said. "But I'm glad you're willing to come. And I know your father would be—"

"Mom, please. I'm gonna come, but you need to stop calling Art my father. He's your husband. He's not my father."

"I'm sorry, Rick. I wasn't thinking. I understand."

Now he felt awful. But it had to be said. "Well, don't worry about it. How can I reach you when I get into town?"

"I'm sure I'll still be here. You can just park and go to the information desk. They'll tell you how to find me. We're in intensive care."

"I'll be there as soon as I can."

4

Come back to me, Art. Please come back.

She gently took his hand, stroked it with her finger. He felt warm, but he didn't squeeze back. He always squeezed back. Could he even feel her touch?

"How ya doing, Mrs. Bell?"

"Am I in your way?"

"No, stay put. You're fine."

The nurse had the sweetest Southern accent. Her *fine* came out like *fahn*. Leanne looked at her name tag. Holly. She wanted to remember. Holly had been so kind. She picked up Art's chart hanging by the edge of the bed. Leanne watched her eyes. No alarm as she read it, no reaction at all. That was good, wasn't it? She looked back at Art.

His face, the same expression.

At least he still looked like Art. Just had this tiny oxygen line across his nose. Walking past the other rooms, she'd seen so many in intensive care wearing such pained expressions, tubes sticking out in every direction. But he was still Art. That wonderful face. Those soft, tender eyes, closed now. How many times had she gazed at those same closed eyes across from her in bed? She always woke up before Art. Had to, it was her job to fix the first pot of coffee.

Oh, Art, please wake up.

"Everything looks stable," Holly said.

"Do you see any progress?"

Holly smiled, eyed the various machines surrounding Art's bed. "Not yet, but believe me, at this point stable is wonderful." She patted Leanne on the shoulder as she walked out.

Leanne watched her disappear through the doorway, which they always left open. Beside it, through a floor-to-ceiling pane of glass, she could see the main nurses' station. At the counter's end, a little Christmas tree, just like the one she and Art had put on the counter at the store on Wednesday. Wednesdays were always a little slow. But this one especially so. Everyone was out shopping the grocery stores, buying food for Thanksgiving dinner. But she and Art had gotten the store all ready before they'd left for the day, so it would look festive for . . . Black Friday.

That was today. The biggest shopping day of the year.

All their regular customers would certainly have stopped by today. In the past few years, dozens more had come in. Last year, they had made enough by the end of the holiday weekend to come all the way out of the red into the black. She wondered what everyone would think as they came by the store throughout the day. No one was there, not even a sign to explain why. She wouldn't let herself begin to calculate how much money they'd lost.

She looked back at Art's face. Only he mattered now.

Her eyes spent a few moments on each machine, trying to understand the numbers and graphs and blinking lights, wondering what improvement looked like. One of them kept going up and down every few moments. Every time it went down, she tensed. But for all she knew, down was good. She'd have to ask Holly to explain all this.

The last machine stood next to the window. Just outside, beyond this dark room, a beautiful blue sky. Soft clouds, whiter than snow, billowed up toward the sun. On the left, a cluster of palm trees swayed, moved by a gentle west wind. Art loved the palm trees most of all.

That and the ocean.

And the sunsets.

Then there were the birds, so many different kinds. The gulls gathered like a flock, but bring out the popcorn and it was every man for himself. The sandpipers running along the water's edge, like Leanne, trying not to get their feet wet. And the pelicans: on the fishing pier they were mischievous thieves. But a sheer delight to watch as they glided like surfers along the wall of the waves.

Art loved it all. And so did she.

She loved being with him the most. Walking with him along the beach, talking, dreaming, praying, even singing (if no one was around). "All it has to be to qualify is a joyful noise," he'd say after they finished destroying a melody. Choir rejects, both of them. But there was no one she'd rather sing praises with than Art. He was a godly man, through and through.

Lord, don't take him yet. I'm not ready. I'm not.

Suddenly she heard footsteps behind her, walking quickly. Before she could turn around, a man in white swept by, behind the bed toward the wall. "I'm sorry, Mrs. Bell, but I need to close these." It was Dr. Halper. He pulled a cord. The drapes rolled shut, plunging the room in almost total darkness.

"What's the matter?" It took a few moments for her eyes to see his face.

He came around to her side of the bed. "I'm sorry if I startled you," he said. "It's just the tests we ran earlier are pointing toward a different diagnosis."

"I don't understand." She looked at his eyes. He didn't seem upset.

"We don't think your husband suffered a stroke." He was talking quietly.

"Then what—"

"We still have a few more tests to run, but we believe he suffered an aneurysm. That's why I closed the blinds. There's a few more things I need to go over with you, some critical things we'll need to do over the next few days."

"Is that worse than a stroke?"

"Both are very serious."

"Life threatening serious?"

He paused. "I'm afraid so. But Art is holding steady." He looked up, glanced at each machine. "For now we're doing fine. The nurse will come in a few moments to change some of his meds."

"What can we do?"

"We're doing everything we can do. But with an aneurysm—until we have more to go on—we've got to keep him very calm. No loud noises, no lights. And absolutely no visitors."

"No visitors?"

"You can stay, but only you. And you need to do your best to stay calm."

"But he can't even hear anything, can he?"

"Probably not. But we'll be working to reduce the swelling in his brain over the next few days. He could wake up at some point. When he does, it would be great if you were here to keep him calm."

"I'm not going anywhere."

"I'll have an orderly bring in one of these nice recliner chairs we have. When you stretch them out, they're not half bad to sleep in. I've done it myself many times."

"How long before we know if he's getting better?"

She didn't like how the doctor's expression changed. He walked over to the chair she had been sitting in. "You better sit down."

She felt faint.

"This thing is going to take time," he said. "Art is in critical condition. What we'll be trying to do over the next several days is to get him ready for surgery."

"What kind of . . . ?"

"Brain surgery. The aneurysm is in his head."

"Oh, Lord." Tears filled her eyes. She looked over at Art lying there so peacefully. "Is this surgery usually successful?"

Another long pause. "In my experience, with this kind of trauma, we really can't predict very much. Wish I could give you more to go on." He reached over and patted her hands. "Right now . . . all we can do is take things one step at a time."

5

Aided by the soothing sounds of Christopher Cross, Carole King, and James Taylor, Rick's sanity arrived mostly intact after the long drive down to Florida. He was glad he was alone; he'd have made terrible company. All he wanted to do was complain.

For starters, this had to be the most boring stretch of highway in the country. It felt like he'd watched the same fifty pine trees roll past the side windows, over and over again, as if on some looping film reel, like those old movies from the forties. Every ten minutes, a meaningless billboard inserted itself into the scene, offering pecans, Indian River fruit, or a cheap roadside motel. (Did anyone even know what Indian River fruit was?) The road never curved. Not a single hill.

Darkness had crept in by inches over the last two hours, creating a new looping film reel. This one played out straight ahead. Two lanes of dimly lit highway, fading toward a black tunnel. Except for the moving yellow lines, it remained a static scene.

Finally, Rick had reached the end of the nothingness. An exit ramp, just off I-95.

He was in familiar territory now: Seabreeze, Florida. A quiet beachside community nestled along the Atlantic, somewhere between Jacksonville and Cape Kennedy. Only a few tourists visited Seabreeze each year, the ones who preferred doing absolutely nothing with their vacation dollars except sitting on the beach.

Rick looked across the street at a 7-Eleven. Must be new. He looked at his dashboard clock and shook his head. Should have been at this spot over an hour ago. It was ridiculous driving fifty-five mph on an interstate highway. When were they going to repeal this stupid law?

He drove through the light and pulled up to the store. The hospital was only ten minutes away, but he was hungry. He'd skipped dinner, hoping to make better time. 7-Eleven hot dogs really weren't half bad. He drove past the pumps and pulled into a slot near the store. He was down half a tank, but he wasn't about to pay $1.15 a gallon, not when he could still get it for 99 cents across the Georgia border. He was only going to be here a few days. A half tank should be plenty.

That was another thing that bugged him: paying over a dollar for a gallon of gas.

In a country that produced as much oil as the United States did, it was an outrage. Four years ago, he'd voted for Carter. The first election he'd paid any attention to. Now gas was up. Inflation was up. Interest rates—this was downright obscene—were at 13 percent. He'd paid 13 percent on his condo in downtown Charlotte. Besides the lousy economy, every morning he had to sip his coffee hearing about the Iran Hostage Crisis . . . *Day 387. Iran Hostage Crisis. Day 388* . . . Today, as soon as he turned on his car . . . *Iran Hostage Crisis. Day 389.*

He opened the door and walked inside the 7-Eleven. Maybe the new guy, Reagan, could do something about all this. But he didn't see how a bad actor would fare any better than a peanut farmer. In any case, this time he hadn't voted for either one.

"Evening, sir." A teenager at the end of the counter smiled then returned to his broom.

Rick nodded, stepped up to the glass container. A dozen hot dogs spun on little rollers; he tried not to think about for how long. He knew the real reason for his lousy mood. It wasn't the president, the gas prices, or the Iran Hostage Crisis. It was being here. Not at the 7-Eleven. Back here in Seabreeze. Facing all this.

His mom, her crisis.

He should have been on the slopes all afternoon.

"Want a hot dog?"

"Yeah. I'll take two." About now, his friends were all sitting around a stone fireplace wearing sweaters, drinking White Russians, holding wooden bowls of steaming hot chili, cooling it down with fresh sourdough bread.

"Here you go."

Rick looked down at his hot dogs wrapped in foil. "Thank you." He walked over to the condiment area. Squirted a thick line of yellow mustard down each one. "Got any relish packs?"

"All out."

Figures, Rick thought. "How 'bout a Slurpee?"

Barely home ten minutes, and look at him.

6

The Seabreeze Medical Center. All three stories of it. He pulled into the oval driveway that wrapped around a three-angel fountain. Rick didn't notice any new wings protruding from either end of the building. It looked exactly as he remembered. When was that? That's right, the eighth grade, a broken collarbone.

He pulled into the visitors' parking lot. Only a smattering of cars. Probably past visiting hours. He walked up the stone stairway on the left side, gliding his hands along the iron rail, admiring the building's architecture. Funny, he'd never given it a thought at fourteen, but it really was amazing, could easily pass for a Spanish mansion or small castle.

He pushed through the glass doors, saw a dark wooden counter across the lobby. An information sign hung from the ceiling tiles. He walked through a thick dome of flowery perfume and found an elderly woman in a striped smock, her face buried in a book. "Excuse me, ma'am."

"Hmmm?" She turned and smiled, set the book down. "How can I help you, young man?"

Rick looked down a long hallway running on the left. He remembered the elevators were down there. "I need to see my mother. She's in intensive care. Well, she's not, her husband is."

"I'm afraid you're forty-five minutes past visiting hours."

"She's not a patient. I just need to speak with her. Her husband had a bad stroke this morning. She's probably in a waiting room close to intensive care."

"I can call there and see."

"Would you please try? I've driven all the way from Charlotte."

She slid her chair across a plastic mat and dialed a number, then began flipping through some papers stapled together. He could hear it faintly ringing, over and over, but no one picked up. "Let me try the nurses' station." After a few rings, a click. "This is Doreen down at the information desk. I've got a young man here who'd like to see his mother, if at all possible." She listened a few moments. "No, she's not a patient. His father's the patient." She looked up at Rick. "What'd you say your mother's name was?"

"It's Bell, Leanne Bell. Her *husband's* name is Art Bell."

Doreen relayed the information. "That's okay," she said in reply. "I'll wait right here." She covered the mouthpiece and said, "They're going to go get her. The nurse confirmed your mom is in the room with your father."

"I'm sure she's going to want to see me. She was pretty frantic when she called."

"Tell you what, just go on up the elevator, down the hall there on the left. Intensive care is on the third floor. They'll have to buzz you in, but I'll tell her you're on your way."

"Thank you."

Rick walked down the long carpeted hall, found the elevators about halfway. Didn't see another soul. Probably just a skeleton crew on duty because of the holiday. When the elevator reached the third floor, his stomach started to tense. He stepped out and found the glass doors blocking the hallway, the entrance to intensive care. He pressed the intercom button and gave his name. One loud buzz and he was through.

He hated hospitals, everything about them. Especially the smell. He kept his gaze straight ahead as he walked along a curving hallway. To his left were floor-to-ceiling glass panels leading to the various rooms. He knew there were beds inside them and lying on them were people, all dying or about to die. He heard clicking sounds and little beeps going off at different intervals.

Who could work at a place like this?

Just up ahead to the right was the nurses' station. A tall middle-aged woman in white stepped out from behind it and walked his way. "Mr. Bell?" she asked in a whisper.

"No, my name's Denton, Rick Denton. My mom's married name is Bell."

"So, Mr. Bell is not your father?"

"No, I just came to see my mother. She asked me to. I just came in off the highway from Charlotte."

"Your mother is the sweetest thing. If you don't mind, could you go back through those glass doors? The first door on your left is our waiting room. We need to keep your father's—I'm sorry—your stepfather's room very quiet. I'll get your mother and tell her to meet you there."

"Fine," Rick whispered back. "Thanks."

He did as instructed and took a seat in the waiting room. A few moments later he heard the glass door open then footsteps. He looked up at the doorway just as his mom walked in. She looked exhausted; her eyes were red. She rushed toward him and started to cry. He held her for a few moments, patting her back. "It'll be all right," he said a few times.

She regained her composure a bit then looked up at his face. "Thanks for coming."

"You don't have to thank me," he said. He led them to the

row of chairs. "Have a seat and tell me . . . what's the latest news? What are the doctors saying?"

She started from the beginning of the day, when she'd first gotten the call about Art being found at the store unconscious. Then walked right through the events of the entire day, providing more detail than he cared to hear. But talking seemed to help, so he didn't hurry her. He grew more alarmed when she shared about the aneurysm development and the anticipated surgery. It wasn't so much the added danger for Art but the added amount of time she was hinting that he'd need to stick around.

"So, you're saying the doctor wants you here at his bedside . . . the whole time?"

"Pretty much, that's what he said."

"For how long?"

"We don't know just yet. I'm sure we'll know more tomorrow."

"More than a few days?" he asked.

"Sounds like it. Oh, Rick, I'm so scared." Tears began to form again.

"It's okay, don't get yourself all upset again. I've got the whole weekend off, including Monday."

She looked down.

"What?"

"I'm afraid I might need you longer than that." She looked up. "Is there any way you could stay longer? I've just got Andrea to work at the store. But this time of year it takes all three of us to keep up. And she's only part-time."

"You want me to work . . . in the store?"

"I didn't mention that?"

"No, you didn't."

"I'm sorry, Rick. But . . . I don't know who else to call."

"I don't know anything about running a store. I don't know any of your . . . merchandise."

"It's mostly just books and music albums, some small gifts. Andrea knows the inventory really well. She could help you."

"I'm not sure how much more time I could get off." He knew that was a lie. He had over three weeks of vacation time saved up for the last two months of the year. All pegged for skiing trips.

"Any time you could spare would be such a help. I can't leave Art. And if we have to close the store now, at this time of year . . ." She looked down. "We always count on the Christmas season to pay all our bills. Art says we make more than 50 percent of our income between Thanksgiving and Christmas."

Rick sighed. This was quickly becoming a nightmare.

She started sobbing, almost uncontrollably. For a moment, he just sat there looking at her. He reached his hand out and put it on her shoulder. "I'll see what I can do. Let's don't worry about it now."

She reached for his hand and squeezed, then looked up. "Thank you, Rick. I'm so sorry to have spoiled your plans. If there was any other way—"

"Don't apologize. What do I need to do?"

She reached for her purse. "Here are my keys. This one here is for the store. We open at 9:00. This one here, with the octagon shape, is for our house."

"Just take the store key off the chain. I've made reservations at the Howard Johnson's, the one on the beachside."

"I don't want you to spend your money."

"It's okay. It's off season, they gave me a great rate. Besides, I haven't seen the beach since I moved away."

"All right," she said, removing the key. "Here." She handed it to him. "I better get back there with Art." They stood up.

Rick added the key to his chain and put it back in his pocket. "You need anything?"

"Not right now. I've already spoken with Andrea. She

normally works on Saturdays anyway, so she should be there when you arrive tomorrow."

"And she knows what she's doing?"

"Pretty much," his mom said, a slight smile appearing. "It's not very complicated, Rick. Nothing compared to what you do every day." She hugged him tightly. "I'm so proud of you. How well you're doing. You know you're the first one in our family to ever get a degree."

"Thanks, Mom. And don't worry. We'll figure this out. Is this the number I should use to call you, the one on this phone?"

"Yes, just leave a message and I'll call back as soon as I can. Thank you, Rick."

"It's okay." He hugged her again and walked out. As he rode the elevator down, he knew all his hopes and holiday plans were heading in the same direction.

7

Rick had planned to take a walk on the beach at sunrise.

Maybe tomorrow.

At the moment, he sat on one of the padded orange benches in a booth at the Howard Johnson's, hurrying through some scrambled eggs and sausage. In about ten minutes, he'd head over to the store; he hoped Andrea would be there as promised. Howard Johnson's looked just like he remembered, except for the part where he was the only one in the restaurant. He glanced toward the back wall at the ice cream bar, the sign above still boasting "28 Luscious Flavors." A handwritten sign taped below it said: "Sorry, only 13 now."

The hostess who'd greeted him and led him to the table now served as his waitress. It appeared that Rick's tip would form the bulk of her morning salary. He saw one old fellow wearing the traditional orange and blue HoJo hat, working by himself in the kitchen. November was typically a slow season, but this seemed a little nuts. Last night the guy at the front desk told Rick things were tough at Howard Johnson's all over the country. Gas prices had slowed tourist travel to a crawl. Last year, the Johnson family sold the whole chain to some British outfit.

There were only four other people staying at the Motor

Lodge. It was kind of sad. Howard Johnson's had been his father's favorite motel. They'd stayed at three of them when they moved down here from Ohio, when Rick was eight. As soon as he'd see a billboard saying it was one mile away, Rick would stick his head out the window like a hound dog. His mom would yell at him to get back inside. He'd let out a shout the moment he saw that bright orange roof sticking out in every direction, the weather vane pointing at the sky. Two wonderful things came next: ice cream and a swimming pool. All the Howard Johnson's had them.

A kid's dream.

Best of all, his dad always made sure they got a room with Magic Fingers. His mom hated that. But he and his dad would lie there, popping quarters in the little gray box every fifteen minutes. The bed would rattle and shake, and their teeth would chatter away. Couldn't fathom now what was so fun about it. It just was. It was a perfect way to end a long day on the road.

Rick smiled, thinking about last night. The Seabreeze HoJo still had three rooms with Magic Fingers beds. One of them faced the ocean, cost five dollars more. The Magic Fingers bed still only cost a quarter. So Rick had just laid there, unwinding, trying to remember when his dad was still with them. Before his mom had run him off two years later.

That was the conclusion he'd come to, but, actually, he wasn't really sure what happened. His mom would never talk about it. But he remembered that he'd had a great dad for a while, and that he was a lot of fun to be with. And he had a mom who seemed mostly concerned about doing the right thing. Bedtimes, vegetables, and chores. Toward the end, he'd hear them yelling behind closed doors, seemed like every night. He could never hear what they said, but it was clear his dad just couldn't take it anymore.

One night, he'd just gotten up and walked out. Rick had

called out to him, chased him out the door. But he sped off down the road. Rick had run down the sidewalk until his dad drove out of sight.

It was the last time Rick saw him.

"You want a refill on that?"

Rick heard the words, but they didn't connect. "What?" he said, looking up at the waitress.

"Want me to top off your coffee?"

He glanced at his watch. "No thanks, I gotta get going."

Their ice cream might be luscious, but the coffee was just awful.

Rick thrummed the dashboard and looked at the clock. He would be at least five minutes late to the store. He was stuck on a little drawbridge, waiting for this sailboat to mosey on by, as cars backed up for blocks on either side. The bridge tender had started opening the bridge when the guy was half a mile away. He couldn't be going more than five mph, sitting on deck sipping his morning coffee, stopping traffic all the way down the intercoastal waterway.

Rick put his car in park; it was obvious he was going to be there a while. He barely noticed the red and silver garland wrapped around the lampposts like a barber pole. The fake boughs of holly tied just below the light fixtures, like Christmas bow ties. He looked beyond the railing toward the big houses lining the water's edge. They were really something. He remembered doing a term paper about them back in high school.

Most were built in the 1920s. Big sprawling affairs. Wrap-around porches. Manicured lawns and hedgerows. The riverfront estates of the rich and famous. They'd escape the snow and ice for a few months then head back north in the spring, leaving a small staff behind to swat mosquitoes and fight the summer heat. The crash of '29 forced most of them into foreclosure.

They fell into disrepair from the 1930s through to the '60s, right up until the mass production of central air-conditioning. That's what Rick's paper had been about: "How Central Air-Conditioning Created the State of Florida."

Rick smiled. Got an A minus. Teacher wrote a little note: "This could have been an A plus if you'd checked your spelling."

Now those same riverfront homes were owned by doctors and lawyers and commercial real estate developers who could live in them all year long, cool as can be. And whenever they pleased, they could shove off the dock in their big sailboats and cruise up and down the river, mocking the rest of mankind.

Suddenly, the guy behind him honked his horn. Rick jumped like someone had smacked him in the head. He looked up. The bridge was down. Cars were moving again. "All right, all right," he said, gave a brief wave.

The bridge dumped the traffic onto the old downtown section of Seabreeze. If you took away the sun and palm trees, threw in some snow and old-timey cars, it looked just like the streets George Bailey ran down in *It's a Wonderful Life*. What was the name of that town . . . Bedrock something. *No, you idiot, that's the Flintstones.* What was it? Bedford Falls. That was it. He turned left at the second light.

Right up ahead was St. Luke's. Same as it ever was. He could see the familiar little sign in the corner sticking out over the sidewalk: The Book Nook. He drove past McAlister's, then a liquor store, a lamp store, a closed-down shoe repair shop, and a women's apparel store, which brought him to the intersection across from St. Luke's. He wondered how many of these stores would be here six months from now when the mall opened up out by the highway.

He'd seen what the mall phenomenon was doing all across the country. He thought it was a wonderful thing.

———▲———

Rick walked down a handful of steps and through the front door. An attractive brunette looked up from the counter and smiled. She had thick, wavy hair tied back with barrettes. She wore a white, Christmassy sweater and blue jeans. "You must be Andrea," Rick said.

"I am." She smiled even wider at the mention of her name. "You must be Rick." She stepped toward him, holding out her hand.

It was soft. Some jewelry but no wedding ring.

"So sorry to hear about your father," she said, her face shifting to instant concern. "Any word this morning? I wanted to visit before I came in, but your mom said they weren't allowing any visitors."

Rick chafed at the father remark. He'd have to clear that up in a little while. "Nothing new that I'm aware of." Of course, there might be. He hadn't called his mother yet today. He brushed away a guilty thought, reminding himself of how rushed he'd been that morning.

"I was so shocked," she said. "It came out of nowhere. He seemed fine on Wednesday."

"Strokes are like that," Rick said.

"You haven't heard? They don't think he had a stroke now. They're saying he had a brain aneurysm. That's what your mom said this morning." She walked back behind the counter.

His mom did say something about that, he thought. "She was crying so much last night, I couldn't catch all the details." He hung his jacket up on a coatrack in the corner. "Say, what's with Columbo out there?"

"Excuse me?"

"The guy in the wrinkled raincoat, hanging around the stairway."

Andrea laughed.

Rick did too, then said, "He asked me if I'm the one. I said, 'What do you mean, am I the one?' Then he says, the one that's bringing his Egg McMuffin from now on."

Andrea laughed harder and put her hand up over her mouth in a cute sort of way. "What did you tell him?"

"I told him to beat it before I call the cops."

Her face showed concern. "Oh, you shouldn't have said that." She hurried past him toward the door. "That was JD. He's this homeless guy, really harmless. Your dad's been buying him an Egg McMuffin every morning, for over a year now."

Your dad.

"JD's the one who found him and called 911." She walked outside, calling JD's name. Rick began to follow her, but she turned and came back. "He's gone."

"I didn't know," Rick said. She walked past him and went behind the counter.

"Don't worry about it. I'm sure he'll be back tomorrow. He might even be back in a little while for coffee. That's the routine. He gets an Egg McMuffin and a cup of coffee, then he's on his way."

Or, Rick thought, you tell him to beat it or you'll call the cops.

A better routine.

8

The morning had started off slow. Just a handful of customers by 10:30. Andrea had used the time to help Rick get familiar with the cash register. About the fourth time through, things began to click. Rick had every confidence he'd eventually master this thing, given that he had a master's degree in accounting. He didn't mention this achievement to Andrea, although the urge had presented itself several times.

He knew he'd better figure out the register, because he had no business helping customers. He didn't know where anything was, hadn't read any of the books or listened to any of the albums, and, honestly, didn't care about any of the religious gifts the store sold. What puzzled Rick the most was that the store had any customers at all.

He'd been to the Book Nook a few times back in high school but had never paid attention to how bad it looked. Starting with the uneven steps leading down from the sidewalk. No, back up . . . starting with the store's location. Stuck in the basement of an old church building in the dying, downtown section of Seabreeze. An area that had become a gathering place for transients and the homeless more than tourists and shoppers.

Like that JD guy, who did come back a few minutes after Rick chased him off. "I forgot to get my coffee," he'd said.

Andrea had poured him a cup, seemed to know exactly how he liked it. Then he was gone. Who needed riffraff like that hanging around the store?

Rick sat on a stool behind the counter. Andrea sat next to him writing something furiously on a pad. She lifted the first page then a sheet of carbon paper and started on a second page. When she finished that, she began cutting the pages with scissors. "What are you doing?"

"A little project for your mom," she said without looking up. "All our customers love your folks. Everyone who hears what happened will want to rush right out to the hospital. I thought I'd write out what happened then cut them up in little notes to give to everyone who comes in."

Rick picked up one of the squares:

Art is very sick in the hospital—an aneurysm.
The doctor said no visitors or phone calls.
Please pray for a miracle.

She was writing this out by hand, over and over. "How many of these you going to make?"

"I don't know. I figured I'd start with fifty, then see if I need more later. While I'm in the aisles helping customers, can you make sure everyone who comes to the register gets one?"

"Sure." He watched her a moment then looked up, did a slow pan of the store. What a dump. The paint was peeling on three walls. The back wall was covered with cheap beige paneling. Bright green Astroturf brought some color into the room. In the main aisle, two seams were joined by duct tape. None of the bookshelves matched. The store was empty.

"Does it ever get any busier than this?" he asked.

Andrea looked up. "It will. About a half hour from now, it'll probably be nonstop until we close. That's why I'm doing this now. Saturdays get pretty busy, usually just before lunch.

But today we'll probably be swamped because of the Thanks-giving sales. You think you can handle the cash register now?"

"I think so." Rick looked down at the keys, tried to men-tally repeat the steps she'd shown him. He'd been a little distracted with her standing right next to him. It was more than her looks or even her light perfume. She gave off some-thing he used to call "good vibes."

"With the next few customers I'll stand beside you but let you ring them up."

"I'd like that." Not what he meant to say. "That'll work," he said. She didn't seem to notice his slip about liking to stand beside her.

"Oh my gosh!" Andrea stood straight up. "Your mom would shoot me."

"What's the matter?"

"I forgot the music." She hurried toward the back of the store.

"The music?"

"Your folks always have music playing through the store," she yelled out. "One of them puts it on, usually your mom."

Your folks. He looked at the front door. Still no custom-ers. He heard a scratching sound above and behind him. He turned and saw a little white speaker on a wooden shelf in the corner. A few moments later, music began to play. A group of male singers he didn't recognize began to sing "O Little Town of Bethlehem." Not his cup of tea, but the harmonies weren't half bad.

"That too loud?" Andrea asked. "It's the new Christmas album by the Imperials."

"Maybe a little."

"How's that?"

"Maybe you better come back. I don't know what you're used to."

"Be right there."

She came out of the little corner office and walked down the center aisle. She really was an attractive woman, and he loved the brightness in her eyes. When she reached the counter, her expression changed.

"What's wrong?"

She came behind the counter and reached for a tissue. "They should be here now . . . your parents. I'm so worried about Art. And your mom must be so scared, poor thing. Never met anyone who trusts God more than her, but—" She wiped tears from her eyes.

He wanted to comfort her somehow but felt a tad hypocritical. He hadn't thought of either one of them since he'd come into the store. Except to get annoyed every time she talked as if Art was his father. "Have they told you much about me?"

"What?"

"My mom and Art, they ever talk about me?"

"Sometimes. I know they're very proud of you."

"How do you know that?"

"When they talk about you, about your job there in . . . where is it?"

"Charlotte."

"Right, at that big CPA firm."

He found this hard to believe. "You said *they*. Art too?"

She nodded. "I think he's your biggest fan."

"You're kidding." Clearly, she wasn't.

"That surprises you?"

"I guess it does. We've never really been that close, Art and me."

"You call your father Art?"

"He's not my father." He tried to say it politely, restraining his annoyance.

"He's not? I had no idea."

"My mom and real dad split up when I was ten. She married Art a few years later."

She paused, seemed puzzled. "Did you go live with your dad?"

"No."

"It's none of my business, I'm just wondering why you and Art aren't close. I mean, if you didn't live with your dad, you must have lived with your mom and Art quite a while."

"I did, up through high school." Now he wanted this conversation to end.

"It's just, Art is such a wonderful man. But I guess it must have been hard to get close to him with your real dad around. I can see how that would be difficult for a little boy to sort out. Art has helped me so much. I kinda treat him like a father figure. Hope you don't mind me saying it."

"I don't mind. Actually, my real dad *wasn't* around. I haven't seen him since . . . well, since he and my mom split up."

"I'm sorry." Now she seemed totally confused.

"It's a long story," Rick said, hoping she'd get the hint.

"Well, one thing you said makes perfect sense now. I understand why your mom gets me so well. I've never met anyone like her. When I talk, it's like she knows exactly what I'm thinking. Even if I get tripped up trying to explain myself. She'll say, 'You mean this?' and it will be exactly what I was trying to say. I never knew she'd been a single mom before."

Rick didn't get how this connected. His confusion must have shown.

"I'm a single mom too," Andrea said. "I have a six-year-old daughter named Amy."

"Oh," he said.

"I love her to bits, but sometimes it gets really hard raising her on my own. Half the time I feel like I'm doing it wrong. I'll make some decision, try to be firm, then Amy will get so upset, like I've broken her heart. I try to hold the line, but inside I'm thinking: *Just let her do it*. Last week I was

talking to your mom about an argument I had with Amy on
the way to school, where once again she's asking me to let
her do something, and I had to say no. Amy left the car and
gave me this look, like she hated me. You know what your
mom said?"

Rick shook his head no, feeling quite sure it was the right
answer. He was mainly stuck on the part about her having a kid.

"She looked at me with those sweet eyes, patted my hand,
and said, 'You're going to be fine, Andrea. God put you in
charge of her on purpose. Just remember when you talk to
her, authority doesn't have to be loud, just firm.' I don't know
how, but whenever she talks, she instantly calms me down.
She always knows just the right thing to say. Well, I don't have
to tell you that. You know what she's like."

Andrea continued talking for several minutes, Rick half
listening, nodding, smiling at various points.

"Is something wrong, Rick?" she finally asked.

"What?"

"Your face, it just got an expression that didn't match
anything I was saying. I know that look . . . you stopped
listening, didn't you?"

"No, I was . . . okay, you got me. But I just drifted a second."

"Are you going to at least tell me what pulled you away
from this fascinating conversation?"

Rick smiled. But he couldn't tell her, at least not here,
not now. He was struggling as he mulled over his mother's
so-called wonderful advice. What was it again? *Authority
doesn't have to be loud, just firm.* What a hypocrite she was.
Andrea should have been there during his teen years. He
couldn't think of any at the moment, but he knew there
must be dozens, if not hundreds, of examples of loud, angry
conversations between them.

What a hypocrite.

9

Leanne looked up from her book. She did something that had become a new habit, ever since they'd wheeled Art into intensive care. Every few seconds she'd look at his face, hoping for a flicker of motion: a fluttering eyelash, a change in his brow, even a slight movement in his lips. Then she'd move to the machines surrounding his bed like sentries; her eyes would rotate past each one, checking the numbers for any fluctuations.

But there was no change.

She noticed a slight movement against the wall, a shifting shadow. She turned and looked up.

"Leanne? I'm sorry to disturb you." It was Holly, one of Art's nurses, standing in the doorway. "There's a call for you in the waiting room, a woman named Andrea. You want to take it?"

Leanne stood and looked at Art. "I'll be right there." She set her book down, leaned over, and kissed him on the forehead. "You will come get me if he stirs?"

"I certainly will," Holly said.

"Thanks again for that little book light. I was going bananas sitting there in the dark all day."

"You are most welcome."

"The doctor said he'd stop in around 6:00," Leanne said.

"I'll get you if he comes. I left the receiver next to the phone on the table. You have the place all to yourself."

"You're such a dear, Holly." Leanne hurried down the hall and waited till the glass doors opened. Then hurried in and picked up the receiver. "Andrea?"

"It's me, Leanne. How are you?"

"I'm okay. Art's vital signs are still strong, but he hasn't regained consciousness. It's the hardest thing not being able to talk with him."

"Must be awful. You two are like best friends. Any news at all?"

"They ran some tests a little while ago. Haven't heard the results. The doctor is supposed to be here any minute."

"Then I better be quick," Andrea said.

"How'd it go today?"

"That's why I'm calling. We sold over twelve hundred dollars!"

"You did? That's wonderful. At least, it sounds wonderful. Art always did the bookkeeping." She meant *does* the bookkeeping. That was a big reason why she was so desperate to have Rick come down. She had plenty of friends from church who would volunteer at the store. But she needed someone who could take care of the books. Just in case Art didn't . . . *No* . . . She wouldn't finish that thought.

"All I know," said Andrea, "is it's four hundred dollars more than any other day since I've worked here. We sold all three of those new nativity sets."

"Really? I told Art people would love those things. But they're so expensive. He didn't want to keep too many on hand. We'll have to order more, it's so early in the season. Did he ever show you how to do that?"

"Well, no."

"I'll bet Rick could figure it out. How'd things go with

him, by the way?" Leanne found herself tensing up as she awaited the answer.

"Fine . . . for me anyway. He's easy to be with and, thankfully, a good talker—I don't mean he talks too much."

"Rick was never shy. How was he with the customers?"

"He looked a bit overwhelmed. Stayed on the register most of the time."

"Were there any . . . incidents?"

Andrea laughed. "Nothing serious. The morning went pretty slow, but after that it was one customer after another. I think Rick liked it when it got busy. He seemed to get pretty uncomfortable when it slowed down, especially when some of the regulars came up to pay."

Leanne gasped. She didn't mean to, but knowing Rick, she could just imagine the scene.

"Molly and Fran stopped in, you should have seen him. Especially when they found out he was your son."

"Oh no." Molly and Fran were two elderly sisters from upstate New York. Molly was a widow; Fran had never married. They'd retired years ago and now lived together in a double-wide mobile home. Leanne often thought they should have their own sitcom.

"Molly shouted, 'You look just like your mother.' She marched around the counter, gave him a big hug."

"What did Rick do?"

"That's not the end of it. She reached up and squeezed both his cheeks, like he was a little boy. 'You're adorable,' she said."

"Oh my," Leanne said, laughing.

"His face got so red. Then Fran scolded her. 'Leave him be, Molly. Look, you're making him nervous.'"

"My goodness. How did he handle it?"

"I could tell he hated it. He looked at me like I was supposed to rescue him, but what could I do?"

"Absolutely nothing," said Leanne. There were so many colorful characters who came into the store. People she and Art had grown to love dearly, but there was no way to prepare Rick for this. She hoped it didn't bother him too much. She had no idea how to keep the store open if he backed out. "Did JD show up for his Egg McMuffin this morning?"

"He did. Rick chased him off."

Leanne wasn't surprised.

"I went after him, wanted to explain the situation. JD did come back for his coffee. Not sure what you want to do with this. Can't see asking Rick to keep the Egg McMuffin thing going."

"No. That won't work. I feel bad saying this, but I can't worry about JD right now. You and Rick talk about what to do tomorrow?"

"Didn't Art say something about opening the store up a few hours after church?" Andrea said.

"He did. He was telling people that all week. They all know we aren't open on Sundays, but he thought we could make an exception for the holiday weekend."

"You still want us to do it?"

"What do you think?" Leanne said.

"Rick said he'd come in if I would. He doesn't feel ready to deal with anything except the cash register. I don't have anyone to watch Amy tomorrow, so I'd have to bring her with me."

"That's fine. I know Art would appreciate it." She was happy to hear that Rick was willing to come in.

"You don't mind about Amy?"

"Not at all."

"Leanne?" A voice behind her. Leanne turned toward the doorway. It was Holly. "Dr. Halper is here. He's in Art's room."

"Okay, I'll be right there," she said. "Andrea, have to go. The doctor's here."

"I'll be praying for you. Let me know if there's anything I can do."

"I will."

"And Leanne . . . sometime in the next day or so, maybe I could ask you a few questions about Rick?"

"Sure," Leanne said. "Anything wrong?"

"No, it's just if I'm going to be working with him a while, it might help if I knew a little more about him. He's very different than I imagined, from the few conversations we've had."

"I'd be happy to talk more about it with you." They said their good-byes, and Leanne walked quickly back to Art's room, trying not to think too deeply about what Andrea had said at the end. As she walked in the room, Dr. Halper was standing at the foot of Art's bed, holding his chart up to the light that shone in from the doorway. He flipped a page and wrote something down.

His face looked serious, in a way that made her instantly uneasy.

10

What a nightmare.

Rick had felt out of his element all day. It was exhausting just matching smiles with these people. Really, who smiles that much? Some of them didn't look like they had a thought in their heads. Just constant smiles served up with the occasional "Praise the Lord" and "Thank you, Jesus."

Rick wanted to say just once: "Don't you know—53 Americans have been held hostage in Iran for the last 390 days!" But they'd just say, "Praise the Lord anyway." Or maybe he'd say: "Our economy is in a shambles! Don't you get it? We got double-digit inflation!" But they'd just smile and say, "God will provide."

They couldn't actually be that happy. He was certain of it.

It was just after 6:00 p.m., already dark. He was sitting in his car at the traffic light on Beach Street. He'd never understood why the town fathers called it Beach Street. It was the main road running through downtown, but it was set back from the ocean by at least half a mile. It actually ran right next to the river, which didn't have a beach and wasn't exactly a river, either. Just part of the intercoastal waterway, which ran up and down the East Coast, around Florida into the Gulf of Mexico. Different towns claimed sections of the waterway that ran nearby, calling it this river or that. As it ran by Seabreeze, they called their section the Seabreeze River.

Well, why not?

Rick was planning to turn right at the light, head back across the Seabreeze River to the real beachside area, when a brightly lit building one block down the road caught his eye. It instantly made him smile. The Davis Brothers Toy Store. Half the storefronts between here and there were dark, either closed for the day or out of business. He couldn't tell which. The only people on the sidewalks appeared to be homeless or doing a passable imitation.

When the light turned, he waved the car behind him to pass. What would it hurt to stop in the toy store a few minutes? He didn't have any place to go.

In all the darkness, the Davis Brothers store really stood out. He remembered that it always did at night, but what they did at Christmastime could almost be called a show. The bronze double doors were set kitty-corner at the intersection. Four big windows ran down either side, each bearing lavish displays of Santa's workshop. As Rick stopped at the intersection, he was happy to see nothing had changed.

He got out of the car, stepped past the curb, noticed all the rust on the parking meter. A brass plate covered up the coin slots. It instantly took him back.

Dad, let me do it!

For a moment, he was eight years old, standing in front of the same toy store, just about this time of year. One of the two years all three of them had lived in Seabreeze together, before his dad had taken off.

Might have been this very meter.

He was a little boy again, holding out his hand. "Dad, have any quarters?"

"Give me a sec to get out of the car."

Rick remembered the car, a white Chevy Impala, but he

couldn't quite remember his dad's face. Not exactly, and that really bothered him. His mom hadn't kept any pictures of him around the house when Rick was growing up.

"You're gonna love this store, Rick. It's like toy stores should be, like the one I used to go to as a kid back in Ohio."

Rick ran up to the first window on the right side; all of them were framed in brightly colored lights. "Look, Dad. Santa's elves. They're really moving."

"Aren't they something?" his dad said. "Now get your fingers off the glass, you'll smudge it all up."

Such a scene of wonder.

Three elves were sitting at a skinny table, cheeks all rosy, wearing little red hats. Each worked on a different toy. The first banged a hammer on the head of a large wooden nail. Of course, the hammer never quite made contact. He was making a rocking horse. Beside him, another elf turned a screwdriver into the propeller of a toy plane. The third pretended to work a lathe back and forth, shaping a baseball bat. Rick could feel his dad's big hands resting on his shoulders. He stood a few extra moments staring into the window, enjoying it.

He ran to the next one. Two more elves at work, one making a jack-in-the-box, the other painting a smile on a doll with curly hair. A third one stood, eyeing a clipboard, his arm moving back and forth as though checking off a list.

"See that one there," Dad said, "the one with the little beard and the clipboard? That's the one you wanna be, Rick. He's the one telling everyone else what to do."

Rick walked slowly past the rest of the windows, mesmerized by each scene. The last two were different, made to look like an outside scene. The first had a large painting of Santa's workshop on the back wall. Three elves loaded the same wrapped toys on Santa's sleigh, over and over again. Rick laughed. It looked like they were smacking the sleigh with them.

The last window included old Saint Nick himself sitting on his sleigh, perched on a rooftop. His big red and white arms moved up and down, as though whipping the reins. The two reindeer nearest the sleigh were actually in the window, the rest painted on a side wall, already lifting into the night sky. "Dad, what are their names? These first two? Dasher and Dancer or Comet and Cupid?"

"Got me."

Whoever they were, their antlers bobbed back and forth like they understood Santa's call. Rick looked at the painting, traced the rest of the reindeer to the end. There was Rudolph, his glowing red nose leading the way.

Standing there now, Rick tried to remember the awe and amazement he'd felt being there with his dad. It was nice that Davis Brothers still made the effort each year to put out these displays. Although, seeing them up close, he could tell they were in serious need of maintenance. In the first window, the elf's hammer came down a full inch from the wooden nail. The paint was chipping and peeling on most of the wooden toys. In the last window, Santa's sleeve was torn. You could actually see the gears turning inside as he pulled on the reins.

He turned and headed to the front door. See, that's why it wasn't good coming home for the holidays. Why skiing trips were better. He hadn't thought about his dad for months. And now look. The few positive sentiments he'd been able to dredge up would now be followed by a black hole of negative emotions. Like, where was his dad now? Why did he leave? Why had he never come back all these years or even tried to call?

He knew most kids who'd been abandoned by a parent wound up blaming themselves, but not Rick. The few memories he had of his dad were good ones. Like this toy store visit. They'd had fun. They got along. Rick knew it had to be his mom, something she said or did back then that drove him off. Then a few years later, she went and married Art, ending any chance of them ever getting back together.

He needed a distraction badly. A walk through the toy store might be just the thing. He wondered if they still had that big Lionel train running overhead throughout the store. Steam would pour out of the smokestack, and the whistle even blew at various spots.

Just then Rick heard someone talking loudly across the street. He turned toward the sound. Great. It was Columbo, the Egg McMuffin guy, heading this way, waving his hands in the air as if in the middle of some argument with an imaginary friend. Rick hurried into the store before their eyes met, then stood inside the door until the man walked by.

He'd seen these homeless guys in downtown Charlotte, even talked with a few of them. They were all the same. Useless parasites. They came off as poor and needy, trying to solicit sympathy from hardworking people. Acting as if they'd come to this sad place through no fault of their own, just an overdose of bad luck. Truth was, they didn't want to work. Didn't want to earn their keep or be accountable to anyone. Fortunately, most had left the Charlotte area when the weather started turning cold.

Looked like a bunch of them had come here to Seabreeze.

Guess both the ducks and the loons head south for the winter.

11

JD and Taylor walked along Beach Street past the Davis Brothers Toy Store, arguing over what they'd be serving tonight at the Walker Street Mission. "JD, trust me. It will be leftover turkey, leftover mashed potatoes, leftover stuffing, and all the rest." Taylor said this calmly but with a slight edge. "And I think you'd be wise to lower the volume of your voice. People are staring."

"Let 'em stare," JD said. "They're gonna anyway." He sidestepped around a trash bin then hurried to catch up with Taylor. Taylor had such long legs, he always felt like he was catching up when they walked together. "I'm with you on the mashed potatoes, but that's all. It's Saturday night, and they always serve Salisbury steak, mashed potatoes, and green beans on Saturday night."

"But this week is different," Taylor said. "People always serve leftovers after Thanksgiving."

"That may be," JD said, "but as I recall, you weren't even there Thursday. I sat down with my plate, turned to say hi to the guy on my left. When I turned back, you were gone."

"You know I don't like crowds."

"I don't like 'em any better, but a man's gotta eat. And you just made my point, why they'll be back to Salisbury steak tonight. That crowd that scared you off. All these new people are in town since the winter set in up north. You see 'em, all over the place. Well, they were there Thursday, chowing down something fierce. Went back for seconds after the line thinned out, and guess what? There weren't any. Every tray was empty."

They both stopped at the next intersection, allowing a single car to pass, then crossed the street. "All right," Taylor said. "I concede. But you know most people call it meatloaf, not Salisbury steak."

"I guess we'll have to disagree on that too," JD said. "Everybody knows you use ketchup with meatloaf. Ever see them set ketchup out on Saturday nights? I don't. They serve it up with gravy. That's the difference, smart guy, why I know it's Salisbury steak." Taylor didn't reply. But JD knew that Taylor knew he was right. That was twice in a row. "Look, there's the mission. You gonna stay this time or take off?"

"I'm not sure," Taylor said. "I had my heart set on meatloaf tonight."

JD thought he was serious, but he could never tell with Taylor. He looked up at his face, and Taylor was smiling.

Still, JD had a feeling he'd be eating alone again tonight.

———————▲———————

"Amen."

About fifty folks had said it, all about the same time. Mostly deep voices, because they were mostly men. Small price to pay, JD thought, eating a hot meal here once a week. As best as he understood, three or four churches took turns manning the mission. He didn't remember them all, but they all followed the same format. A team of volunteers set the food out on a line of tables. Then they'd stand around as people wandered in. All the "guests" had to take a seat before anyone could eat. They could talk to each other if they wanted. Some did. Some just stared at the table.

JD wasn't interested in talk. He was there to eat.

After everyone was seated, one of the men from the church would get up, tell everyone how happy he was to see them, and say the blessing. It was nice. Most of the time. Every now and then, someone new came in and prayed way too long, till everyone started to fidget. After they finished praying, the guests all said amen, and it was Salisbury steak time.

JD got up and got in line. Folks usually behaved in line. It was hard, for him anyway, especially when he was starving. About ten men got in ahead of him. He looked around the room. Like he figured, Taylor had split. But he was a good friend, for the most part.

He just didn't like crowds.

"How are you doing tonight? It's JB, right?"

JD looked up. A short, heavyset man about his own age was smiling at him. "Close. JD."

"Sorry, JD." He handed him a tray and some plasticware wrapped in a napkin. "Well, enjoy your dinner."

JD looked down the line, at the next station, the good stuff. Didn't really want to small talk with the help. A smile was in order, a word or two. But JD found that if you looked at them too long, they'd start asking get-to-know-you questions. And the ones who got sucked in that far might have someone sit next to them while they ate. JD had all the company in the world he cared to keep with Taylor.

And Art.

He missed Art.

At first, he thought it was just the Egg McMuffins. But for the last two days, he kept seeing poor Art in his mind, lying there on the floor, not moving. JD had called 911 then bugged out of there before anyone had seen him. Found out later, Art wasn't dead, just in the hospital.

So maybe things would go back to normal.

He didn't want to think about how long that might take. He knew he wouldn't be getting a McMuffin tomorrow, seeing as it was Sunday. But what about Monday? This new guy seemed pretty nasty. Nice of Andrea, though, to come after him like that, offer him coffee. But she was never there except on Saturday. Should he show up on Monday morning and see? He had to stop thinking about it. Or it'd be eating him up every moment till then.

With his tray filled up, JD walked back to the spot where he always sat. Some new guy was in it. JD stood right next to him a few moments, sending a message.

"Lemme guess," the man said, looking up. "Your seat?"

JD nodded.

"No problem, man. Don't want any trouble." He got up and moved two tables away.

JD sat and started eating. He loved Salisbury steak, loved the whole dinner on Saturday nights.

"Okay, folks."

JD looked to the front of the room. He remembered, this guy wasn't bad.

"For you old-timers, you know the scoop. For our newer guests, let me welcome you and tell you what's what."

JD could tell who all the new guys were. They stopped eating to listen.

"My name's Frank Hamilton, one of the elders at Christ Community Church. I'm going to talk to you all about the love of God for the next twenty minutes or so, but please keep on eating or your food will get cold. That's how we do things here at Walker. We won't think you're impolite."

Everyone instantly started eating again. JD was already half done.

"Before I share what God's put on my heart, I just want to draw your attention to the set of tables at the back of the room a moment."

JD heard a bunch of chairs scraping and saw guys turning, but he wasn't about to stop eating.

"We've brought in stacks of donated blankets. Now I know those of you who've lived here a while understand that Seabreeze is mostly a nice stop in the winter, but we're set a little north of center in this great state of ours. So if a serious cold snap hits the southeast part of the country, some of that weather can dip down here a day or two and make life pretty uncomfortable. Well, something just like that's supposed to be blowing in tomorrow afternoon, a cold front. The weatherman is predicting it might even get down in the low thirties or even the high twenties late tomorrow night."

Groans rumbled through the room.

"We're urging you folks to take this seriously. On your way out, please take one of these blankets. There's plenty of them. Some of you who aren't too attached to this place may want to consider heading farther south tomorrow. Get below Melbourne and you should be fine. But if you're staying, you should really come in from outside, stay in one of the shelters. They're first come, first served, so I wouldn't wait too long tomorrow before checking in."

JD shook his head. No way he'd stay in one of those places.

The man continued. "I know some of you diehards are thinking you can tough it out, but I'm asking you to reconsider. We didn't have any freezes here last year, so if you're thinking you did fine last year, trust me, it's not going to be the same." The man paused, looked down at the wooden podium. "I'm not trying to scare anyone, but two years ago, it did freeze here in Seabreeze, and we lost two men to the cold. I don't want that to happen to anyone here tonight. Which might be a good lead-in to what I really came here to share with you."

JD looked down at his plate, scooped up the last spoonful of mashed potatoes, swirled it around a dab of gravy. He'd happily take one of their blankets, could always use a fresh one of those.

But no way he'd be heading in to one of those shelters.

12

"You better sit for this, Leanne."

Lord, help me to not fall apart.

As she sat in the chair, her eyes stayed focused on Dr. Halper's face, looking for any signs of hope. He pulled the other chair close, into a shaft of light coming from the hall, lifting it so it wouldn't scrape the floor. They had moved to the front of the room, away from Art's bed. "Is Art going to die?" she asked quietly. "Is that what you need to tell me?"

Dr. Halper looked down at the floor. He raised his head slowly and said, "I think I'd like to answer that with a fuller explanation than just a simple yes or no."

Okay, she thought, at least he didn't say yes.

"After reviewing the tests and consulting with some other doctors, I think we know better what we're dealing with here, and where we need to go. But I want you to understand the situation, including the risks involved." He picked up a clipboard, pulled some sheets back, and began to draw on a blank page.

Leanne waited patiently, trying to figure out what he was drawing. From her upside-down viewpoint it looked like a tree.

"Art had an aneurysm in his brain." He turned the clipboard

toward her, holding it to the light. "See these, these are like the main arteries in his brain. We all have them." He pointed to a thick line that divided into two smaller ones. At the fork he had drawn a small round circle. "See this," he said, pointing at the circle. "This is the aneurysm—well, it *was* the aneurysm, before it burst."

"Did that happen yesterday?" she asked.

He nodded. "But the aneurysm could have been there much longer. Has Art been complaining of severe headaches lately?"

"No."

"Any speech problems? Any problems with his balance?"

"No."

"Has he been forgetting things?"

Leanne smiled. "Doc, we both have. But that's been going on for years."

Dr. Halper smiled. "I mean more serious things than that. The kind of forgetting that would really concern you."

She shook her head.

"I guess, then, it's possible it could have just formed yesterday. The point isn't the bubble so much, but that the bubble burst."

He went on to explain all the things that had happened in Art's head after that. She was sure he was trying to make it simple, but it was just too much to comprehend. It all sounded so awful. When he finished, she asked, "Was it painful? Did Art suffer before he lost consciousness?"

Dr. Halper reached out and patted her hand. "Hard to say, Leanne. I don't think so. I'd say he lost consciousness pretty quickly. The amazing thing is that it stopped bleeding. An aneurysm that size more often just bleeds out and the patient dies on the spot."

"Oh, Lord."

"In 15 percent of these cases, people die before ever reaching the hospital."

"So that's good, right? I mean, that Art's made it this far?"

The doctor removed his hand and sat up straight. He inhaled deeply and looked at her as though much worse was to come.

"Leanne, I want so much to give you reason to hope, but my job right now is not to do that. I need to help you understand the situation as best as we understand it, so that you can give us an informed consent for what we think needs to happen from here."

Leanne took a deep breath. "Okay, I'm sorry I keep interrupting you. I—"

"Don't apologize. You just want Art to be okay. I want that too." He glanced up at the machines surrounding Art, his eyes spending a moment at each one.

"Go on, Doctor. I'm listening."

"See . . . there's nothing to keep Art's aneurysm from starting up again. For some reason, it just stopped."

"So what do we do?"

"We have to go in and fix it."

"Can you do that?"

"That's part of what we need to talk about. Art's aneurysm is in a very delicate place. After looking at the scans, I believe it's in his best interest to have another surgeon do the operation. I'm good, but I'm not the best. At Shands they have the finest neurosurgeon in the southeast. I've called him and he's willing to look at Art's case."

"Shands is in Gainesville, isn't it? Is the surgeon coming here?"

"No, that won't be necessary. If you approve of this plan, I will authorize a courier to drive Art's file to Shands. The surgeon there will have all the information he needs by midmorning."

Leanne looked up at Art, did that quick routine with her eyes. Of course, there was no change. She wished she could talk to him. He always made the big decisions. "Then what, do you drive Art to Gainesville?"

"Not right away. We'll need to keep him here until the swelling in his brain has gone down."

"How long will that take?"

"Hard to say, a few days, a week."

"But what if he has another bleed before then?"

Dr. Halper shook his head. It was obvious this was very difficult for him.

"I'm sorry, I shouldn't have asked that?"

"No . . . I've asked myself that question a dozen times. It's . . . a risk. That's why we're keeping his room dark and quiet. Why I'm keeping him sedated."

The whole thing felt like it should be overwhelming her. She was surprised at how well she was taking it. Dr. Halper had clearly thought about this very carefully. She'd been praying, asking God to heal Art miraculously, but, if not that, to give the doctor wisdom and direct his thoughts in the right direction. "What will happen once we take Art to Shands?"

"They will operate. The surgeon will go right to the aneurysm and tie it off with a clip. After that, the hope is that it won't bleed ever again. And Art will heal up and make a full recovery."

He didn't sound convincing. "That's . . . the *hope*?"

"I've got to be honest with you." He looked away, toward the door. Then turned toward her again. "Hope is the strongest word I can use, in light of what we're facing."

"So after all this, Art could still die?"

"Leanne . . . you need to know. Yes, Art could still die. Earlier I said 15 percent of aneurysm cases die before they reach the hospital. But another 50 percent die within thirty days of reaching the hospital. Of those who survive past thirty days, half of them suffer permanent brain damage."

Leanne closed her eyes. Tears began rolling down her face.

13

No sunrise beach walk today, either.

Best Rick could manage was crawling out of bed at 10:30 a.m. He blamed it on boredom and one too many rum and Cokes last night.

After he'd walked through the toy store, Rick had a hunch he should call his mother before heading back to HoJo's, so he'd stopped at a pay phone. Good thing he did. She was a mess. Through nonstop tears, she'd filled him in on the latest update from the doctor. It sounded pretty bad for old Art.

Sounded pretty bad for him too.

Rick had only planned on staying through today, planned to drive home tomorrow. He was supposed to be back at work on Tuesday. Mom didn't come right out and say it, but it was obvious she was hoping he'd stay on at the store for at least another week. He had plenty of vacation time left. He'd have to be a pretty lousy son not to give in. Didn't see any other way around it.

That conclusion is what led to the "one too many" rum and Cokes last night. He couldn't believe it. Here he was on a Saturday night, sitting in a rundown Howard Johnson's, drinking by himself, watching television. He'd actually sat through an episode of *Trapper John, M.D.* He did learn one important thing: Magic Fingers felt a lot better on your back when you were drunk. Seemed to last longer too.

But that was behind him now. Before him lay the beach, the ocean, the blue sky, and the breeze, for which this town was named. It was hard to fathom it was almost December. He wore a short-sleeved shirt, cutoff jeans, and bare feet. The water was a bit nippy for his taste, but that didn't stop a handful of tourists splashing around in the waves right in front of him. Their skin was vampire white. The ladies wore latex swimming caps and the men wore something way too close to bikini bottoms, their bellies like beach balls bouncing in the sea.

It was revolting. He had to look away.

Actually, thirty minutes into his walk and he just had to wonder why God ever made people in the first place. Everywhere he looked—with people out of the picture—were scenes that inspired wonder and awe. The colors in the sky, the reflections in the water, the rolling sand dunes, sea oats and palm trees. The seagulls and pelicans, sand crabs and periwinkles. It all fit together in harmonious symmetry. Gazing at such things, it was hard not to believe in a Supreme Being.

But if he turned his head just a tad, there were these human beings trampling through the beautiful scenes, looking ridiculous and entirely out of place.

Like the woman walking toward him just now, not twenty paces ahead. She had to be seventy, wearing a bright pink (and skimpy) two-piece bathing suit, her skin all leathery from a thousand hours baking in the sun. On her head she wore a matching pink towel like a turban.

No one should have to see this. Not on a beach handcrafted by Almighty God.

She smiled at him as she passed. He smiled back. Then realized that he must have been staring, sadly reinforcing her delusion.

Not far behind her was a middle-aged man walking at a furious pace. At least he was covered up. But with what? A plaid shirt and striped short pants. And he wore sneakers with dark colored socks—dark colored socks—pulled up to his knees. Who does that? He wore a baseball cap with a white cloth hanging down the back like a mullet. His arms flung way up and down with each step. Obviously for some cardiovascular benefit. But should Rick have to see it?

Should anyone have to see it?

Rick stopped and looked at his watch. He'd better turn around and head back to the motel. He needed to get showered, get something to eat before driving over the bridge to the store. He sat a moment to allow the last two walkers to get far out in front. For a few brief minutes, the beach was clear of human debris. He sat back, resting on his hands, and took in a deep breath of fresh air.

His thoughts drifted back to one of the conversations he'd had with Andrea yesterday. The one where she'd talked about how wonderful his mother was, how she always knew just the right thing to say and always gave out such perfect advice. What was that quote again, the one that really bugged him? Something about authority.

That's right . . . *Authority doesn't have to be loud, just firm.*

He shook his head at the absurdity of the remark. Their relationship, especially during his teen years, was filled with loud arguments. He got up and started walking. As he did, his mind began searching through the files, trying to remember some of the bigger fights. Not so much what the fights were about but the harsh things that were said . . . and the volume.

He kept walking and walking and thinking the whole while.

At one point, he stopped in his tracks. In every memory he conjured up, every loud conversation he could recall with his mother . . . *he* was the loud one, not her. He couldn't remember a single instance when she had actually yelled or raised her voice at him. How was that possible? Until that moment, it had been a settled thing in his mind for years, what he'd always believed.

His mom had been a strict, overbearing parent.

But in every memory he could recall, she really had only ever been . . . firm.

That couldn't be right. He had to be forgetting something.

14

Rick arrived at the Book Nook a few minutes before 1:00 p.m. There were several spots along the curb to park; he pulled his Celica into the one closest to the front door. That way he could watch through the glass doorway window, see if any of the bums hanging around here started messing with it. The lights were on inside. Andrea must have already opened things up.

As he stepped through the doorway, he was surprised to find the store mostly empty. Just a few teenagers looking at records, a gray-haired lady eyeing the knickknacks. Andrea was sitting on a stool behind the counter. Her hair was different somehow, pulled back farther behind her head maybe. It looked nice. She wore a light green sweater. Some Christmas music played through the speakers. Nobody he recognized.

She smiled as he walked toward her. "Didn't bring a jacket?" she asked.

He'd put on a green velour pullover that morning and had wondered if it would be too warm. "Feels pretty nice out there."

"Guess you didn't catch the news. A cold front is blowing in this afternoon. Temperature is supposed to start dropping before dark."

He shook his head. "Forgot about the roller-coaster weather you all get down here in the winter. Maybe it'll be good for business. Make people feel like Christmas shopping." He stood next to her, leaned close so the elderly woman didn't hear him. "Why's the store so empty?"

"I guess the regulars are used to us being closed on Sundays. I didn't tell anyone yesterday that we'd be open, because I hadn't talked with your mom yet. But it might be a good thing if it's a little slow, give us some time to catch up."

He wasn't quite sure what that meant.

"I mean, I probably need to spend some time with you, going over the merchandise, since you'll be on your own tomorrow."

"What?"

"I guess we got so busy yesterday, I forgot to tell you. I can only work in the afternoon. I'm a waitress at a little restaurant over on Beach Street. Just breakfast and lunch, but I usually don't get off till 2:30, sometimes 3:00. So you'll have to open up, hold down the fort on your own till then."

He couldn't believe it. His face must have registered the shock.

"It's not that bad, Rick. Really. I can probably show you everything you need to know in an hour. You'll probably find the most difficult thing will be keeping the coffee going and remembering to turn the music on when it cuts off. I'm going to make some cassettes for you before I leave, so you'll at least have ninety minutes worth at a time."

Rick didn't make coffee. He either bought it or one of the secretaries made it at the office.

"Actually, after I show you what to do in here, I was hoping you might be able to spend some time back in Art's office. We need to order some things so they'll be here by the end of the week."

This was growing more sour by the minute.

"But come here first. There's somebody I want you to meet." She stood up and walked around him. Then a few steps down the center aisle.

He watched her but didn't respond, still reeling a bit from the things she'd just said.

She turned around. "C'mon. It'll just take a minute."

He followed her toward the back.

"Say, Andrea," a male voice yelled over one of the aisles near the front.

They stopped halfway. "Need something?" she replied.

It was one of the teenagers by the records. "We can't find Keith Green's new album. Thought it came out a while ago."

"We don't carry it. None of the stores do," she said. "Guess you didn't hear. He's not selling them in stores anymore. You've got to order it directly from his ministry in Texas."

"Really? Know how much they're selling it for?"

"For free . . . well, not really for free. For however much you want to donate."

"No way. You mean I could get it if I sent in a dollar?"

"I suppose, but I think you're missing the point. When you're ready to check out, I'll give you one of his newsletters. I have a few under the counter."

"Hey, dude," his friend said. "We can both get one, maybe we'll send in five bucks between us."

Andrea continued walking down the aisle. Rick didn't understand a single word of that conversation.

They reached an open area with a sofa and upholstered chair. A little girl sat on the sofa, with some kind of project spread out beside her, with more of it on the coffee table.

"Amy, I'd like you to meet Mr. Denton. He's Leanne's son." The little girl looked up, smiling brightly. She had the same color hair as Andrea, pulled into a ponytail on one side.

"I didn't know Mrs. Bell had a boy."

"Well, he's not a boy, Amy."

"Well, I didn't want to say she had a *man*."

Rick laughed. She was cute. She reached out her little hand, so he shook it. "Nice to meet you, Amy."

"And you too, Mr. Denton."

"Can she call me Rick?" he asked Andrea quietly.

"It's okay with me."

"How about you call me Rick?"

"Okay."

"What you got here, some kind of school project?"

"No, silly." She held up a JCPenney Christmas catalog, with a picture of Santa on the front wearing a blue apron, painting a toy. "I'm making a catalog."

Rick didn't understand. "Looks like the catalog is already made."

She held up a black composition notebook. "No," she gently scolded. "*This* is my catalog. I'm making it for Annabelle, so she can pick out what she wants for Christmas."

He saw a blonde-haired doll sitting next to her on the sofa. Presumably Annabelle. "Oh. Why don't you just have Annabelle look at the Penney's catalog?"

Amy looked all set to explain. "Hold on, sweetie," Andrea said. "You can tell Rick all about that later. I've got some things I need to show him in the store first."

"Okay. It's not ready to show anyone yet anyway. I've got a lot more I have to do with it first."

Andrea headed toward the aisle closest to the back wall. "We'll start over here."

"Okay if I get a cup of coffee first?"

"Yeah, I can use one too. Then we'll make a fresh pot."

"You're going to have to show me how to do that too."

"What?"

"Make coffee. I don't know how."

"You're kidding."

He shook his head. "Accountants don't make coffee."

She smiled. "Guess that means you don't clean toilets, either."

"Toilets?"

"I was saving that for last."

15

Rick sat in the Book Nook's dreary back office, Art's office.

A few minutes ago, Andrea had finished giving him the grand tour, explaining way more than he could retain. But she was right. It wasn't that complicated. He'd actually felt stupid for his apprehension. Teenagers in high school get hired for jobs like this at minimum wage. People came in to the store, picked stuff out, and brought it up to the counter to pay for it. That's it.

But if they asked questions about the merchandise, that would be a problem. *What's the best book on marriage? I'm buying a book for a friend, do you recommend this one? Which of these three Bibles is a better translation?* He didn't know anything, knew he didn't know anything, but he hated appearing that way. He had an almost biological resistance to saying "I don't know." His practice had always been to come up with something that sounded like it made sense and say it with authority.

But he couldn't do that here; he had no reference point to even pretend.

Andrea had seemed to discern his struggle and offered some advice: "If customers ask you questions, tell them you're just watching the store for a few days to help your mom out while Art's in the hospital." Then she walked him behind the counter and pulled out a pad of paper, suggesting he could write their questions down, get their name and phone number, and tell them she'd call them back when she got in at around 3:00 p.m.

Rick had then asked if she shouldn't write down her phone number in case any of their questions were urgent. Immediately, he felt like a total fool for saying it. Who would ever have a question about a religious book that needed immediate attention? She'd given him a look that said "You're kidding, right?" But she didn't say it, which was all he could hope for. Instead she'd said, "I can't take personal calls at the restaurant."

Rick knew he'd only asked the question to get her telephone number. Like some reflex reaction. Thankfully, she didn't seem to detect his scheme. She was probably wondering, though, how someone with a master's degree could ask such a lame question.

Sitting there now in Art's squeaky chair, he looked back on this whole episode with a fair amount of self-disdain. Because, after all, he wasn't interested in Andrea, so there was no point responding to some misguided impulse to get her phone number. She was attractive enough, more than a little, and had a pleasing personality . . . and she smelled nice.

But she was a churchgoer, like his mom.

Worse than that . . . she had a kid.

———— ▲ ————

Andrea popped her head through the office doorway. "How's it going back here?"

Rick looked around at the mess of papers and stacks of folders. "Not so good. I'm sure Art had some kind of system here, but I'm not seeing it yet." She had given him a written list of books, records, and religious paraphernalia to reorder, hoping to get them in the store and ready for resale by this Friday. Almost two hours had passed. "So far," Rick said, "I've only found three of the wholesale vendors who sell the items on your list."

"Any of them those big nativity sets?"

Rick shook his head. "Nope."

"Hope you find them. I've had several people asking about them. Think your mom said they had a really nice markup." She looked around the office. "Wish I could help you, but I hardly ever did anything back here."

"I'm sure if I keep digging, I'll connect all the dots. No customers out there?"

"Not at the moment. Care for a cup of coffee?"

"I'd love one."

"Feel like making it? What's left in here doesn't smell very good."

Rick made a face.

"I know you watched me make the last pot, but tomorrow you're going to have to tackle this giant on your own."

Rick smiled then got up. At about the same time, the front door opened and closed. "Better see who that is," she said. "Sure you're okay?"

He wanted to say "It's just coffee." But he was a little nervous. "I remember what you did. Just not sure how it'll turn out."

"We're not Dunkin' Donuts, so if it's close, most people will be fine." She smiled then walked away.

He got up and walked the few steps to the little cabinet next to the sofa, where the Mr. Coffee sat. As he began carefully following the steps he'd just committed to memory, he remembered reading an interview with the inventor of Mr. Coffee in a *Forbes* magazine article last year. The guy compared his creativity to that of Michelangelo. It was a clever little thing. But c'mon . . . it just made coffee.

He glanced over at Amy still hard at work on her catalog project. She looked up at him. "I like that smell."

"Me too. Like how it tastes?"

"I'm only six."

Rick laughed. "Right." He needed to stop talking so he didn't screw up the count on the scoops. Out of the corner of his eye, he could tell she was still looking at him.

"Sorry about your dad," she said. "I mean, your stepdad. I really like Mr. Art. He's so nice to my mom and me. Sometimes I pretend he's my grandpa, and your mommy is my grandma. It's easy because they act just like grandparents are supposed to. Your mommy always gives me Chiclets gum from her purse. Both of them always give me big hugs when they see me, and more hugs when I have to go."

Rick kept his eye on his assignment. It didn't seem like Amy required anything from him to keep the conversation going.

"Sometimes after school I have to come here, because my friend Jenny's mom can't watch me. Sometimes Mr. Art sits right here beside me and reads me Bible stories. Did he ever read you stories when you were a kid? He always smells nice. Like flowers for men. Hope he feels better soon."

Rick smiled. At least she wasn't a brat. He listened for, then heard, the appropriate gurgling sound, bent over to watch the black drips as they started spilling into the pot. He had a few minutes, so he walked over and sat down beside her. "You almost done with your catalog?"

"Almost," she said. "There's just a few more things Anna-belle might want for Christmas." She had the Penney's catalog opened up on the coffee table. The toy section was all cut up. "Like Baby Softina." She pointed at a doll then turned the page. "And Holly Hobbie, the little one here that looks like a baby." She turned a few more pages. "This Easy-Bake Oven." She flipped several pages. "And this Miss Piggy doll. I think when I cut these out I'll be all done with my catalog."

"Can I see it a minute?" he asked.

"Sure." She handed Rick the Penney's catalog.

He flipped it forward a few pages. "The Empire Strikes Back," he said. "Did you see this? Look at these action figures, Luke Skywalker, Chewbacca, Han Solo . . . look at this *Millennium Falcon*. It's just like the one in the movie. I would have loved that as a kid. How come you didn't cut these out?" Of course he was kidding.

"Because Annabelle doesn't want things like that. They're for boys."

He handed the catalog back to her. "Can I see that?" He pointed to her handmade one. She gave it to him. "So Annabelle wants everything in here?"

"Well, she may want all of it, but she won't get all of it."

"Why not?"

"That's not how it works, silly. You ask for some stuff, but you don't get most of what you ask for. Maybe one or two things . . . and never the thing you want most."

"What does Annabelle want most this year?"

"Can I see it?" she asked. Rick gave it back. She turned to the first page. "Barbie's Dream House," she said, "with all the furniture." Her face lit up as she pointed to the cutout picture. She closed her eyes a moment, then sighed. She pointed to the second page. "And the Barbie Super Vette here."

He noticed that none of the toy pictures in her catalog had prices; she'd cut around them. "So . . . why does Annabelle want a catalog with so many things in it if she knows she's only going to get one or two presents?"

"Because . . . it's lots of fun to look, and girls love to look at stuff."

Rick laughed. "But if this is kind of a make-believe catalog, why can't Annabelle ask for the thing she wants the most?"

Amy shook her head. "Because what you want the most is always too expensive."

Rick realized . . . they really weren't talking about Annabelle anymore.

16

"Thanks for checking in, Rick. But there haven't been any changes with Art. Of course, they tell me that's a good thing. The whole idea is to keep him calm, get him ready for surgery." Leanne looked at the waiting room clock. It was a few minutes after 7:00 p.m. From the other end of the phone, Rick filled her in on what he'd done in the office. He'd finally figured out how to order everything on Andrea's list, but he was just getting out of the store now, two hours after it closed.

"Wish I could help you, Rick, but I don't know what Art does back there. I'm so sorry you have to use vacation time like this."

"It's all right, Mom. They say when they're moving him to Shands?"

"I'm not sure. Maybe in a day, maybe two."

"And after that . . . what?"

"I guess the surgery. I don't know if they'll do it right away or wait and see how he does once he gets there." Leanne could almost feel the next question coming and hoped he didn't ask. Something about how long it would take for Art to recover after the surgery. Rick had probably figured out it would stretch into next week, if not longer. He'd be wondering how much longer he'd have to stay and help. If he asked, she didn't know what to say. Dr. Halper didn't even know where things were going yet. She couldn't think about next week. It was all she could do to get through each day.

"So," Rick said after a pause, "guess I better let you go. Oh . . . hope you don't mind, but we had to turn the heat on at the end of the day."

"That's okay. I haven't been outside, but Andrea stopped by a little while ago. She dropped off my coat and a few things. She said it's supposed to freeze overnight."

"There goes my midnight swim."

She laughed. He always did have a good sense of humor. She suddenly felt bad for judging him. Maybe he wasn't thinking the things she was afraid he was thinking. She just didn't know who else to turn to if he went back to Charlotte now. But she also knew he couldn't stay. He had an important job, his own life to live.

"Might need to get that heater looked at," Rick said. "It was louder than the Christmas music."

"Art's been asking our landlord to replace it for two years," she said.

"Who's the landlord?"

"The congregation upstairs, at St. Luke's. But there's less than a hundred attending every Sunday, so the money's just not there."

"Not a big deal," he said. "Least it works."

"Did you bring a jacket?" she asked. She heard him chuckle on the other end. "I'm always going to be your mom."

"Actually, I didn't. Wasn't watching the weather, but my car is just five steps from the door. I'll bring a jacket tomorrow. Need anything before I head to the motel?"

"No, Andrea took good care of me. But . . . now that it looks like . . ." How should she say this?

"What's the matter?"

"I just feel bad, you staying at a hotel when our house is

sitting there empty every night. Your room, it's just the way you left it. There's food in the fridge that's probably going to go bad in a few days. When you came down on Friday, you were thinking it was just going to be the weekend. You're welcome to stay."

"I know, Mom. But I like being on the beach. Makes it feel more like a vacation. And with what I make now, it's really . . . not a problem."

"Just had to check. Thanks again, Rick. You have no idea how much it helps having you here."

"Take care of yourself," he said, and then hung up.

That didn't go so bad, she thought as she walked back toward Art's room.

"Leanne?"

Leanne turned around. It was Holly, walking from the nurses' station, holding a small box. "Got something for you."

"What is it?"

She handed her the box filled with dozens of pink pieces of paper. "Didn't know we had a celebrity in the ICU."

"What are these?"

"The phone's been ringing nonstop all day at the information desk. People asking about Art. We couldn't put them through to the ICU waiting room, so they asked the auxiliary volunteers to just take down the messages."

Leanne smiled, looking at them all. "Thank you." She walked back to his room. How wonderful. Art would be so happy to see this. She sat down in her chair with the box on her lap.

If only he could see it.

She felt a chill sitting there near the window and got up to get her coat.

Andrea turned the light out in the living room of their little garage apartment. She didn't know if the temperature had dropped below freezing outside, but it must have in here. She looked down at Amy, already asleep, bundled in blankets on the sofa, which doubled as her bed. It was just a one-bedroom place. Amy had asked if she could start sleeping out here a few months ago. Andrea finally got her to admit that someone at school had made fun of her when they'd heard she slept in her mother's room.

Andrea wished she could afford a two-bedroom place, but she didn't even make enough to run the heat on nights like this. Last year, she'd forgotten to turn the thermostat down a few cold winter nights and got the shock of her life when she'd opened the electric bill.

She walked out to the kitchenette and glanced at a thermometer on the wall. Sixty-one degrees, it said. How was that possible? Felt like thirty-something in here. She felt a pang of guilt when an image of JD flashed into her mind, then some of the other homeless people she saw every day downtown. What did they do on nights like this?

She felt restless. She wasn't sleepy. That was the unfortunate trade-off of letting Amy sleep in the living room. It meant no television for Andrea after 8:30 p.m. After dinner, they had watched *The Wonderful World of Disney* together, which they both loved, then *Mork & Mindy*, which Amy loved and Andrea couldn't stand.

Nanu nanu. Like fingernails on a chalkboard every time she heard it.

She poured herself a glass of milk then turned the lights out in the kitchen and walked into the bedroom, the coldest room in the apartment. She set the milk down on a table beside the bed and looked around. She'd have to find a way to get the television in here. She quickly changed into her flannel pajamas and put on her bathrobe. It would stay on all night. Then she all but ran to the bed and slipped under the covers.

She reached for the book she'd been reading the last few

nights, one Art had recommended. It was Hannah Hurnard's *Hinds' Feet on High Places*, a wonderful allegorical tale first written in 1955. Art said it was destined to be a classic. The main character was a young woman named Much-Afraid who lived in the Valley of Humiliation with her terrible relatives the Fearings.

Andrea got it, right off, why Art had recommended this book. Her life was plagued with fears. She wasn't like Much-Afraid. She *was* Much-Afraid. She wanted to learn all the lessons the Chief Shepherd sought to teach Much-Afraid in the book. How to develop "hinds' feet" so one day she could easily jump and skip to the High Places, unshackled from all her fears.

Andrea looked at her tiny bedroom, only half-lit by the lamp. She wasn't there yet. Not even close. She definitely still lived in the Valley of Humiliation. And the Fearings were all around her.

———— ▲ ————

JD could see his every breath.

Before bending over and crawling inside his box, he'd looked up. Not a single cloud in the night sky. Had to be after 1:00 a.m. by now. He huddled against the back of the box, as far from the opening as he could, his knees drawn tight against his chest. He had on his overcoat and wrapped himself in the blanket he'd gotten from the mission. If the blanket was helping, he couldn't tell. The box itself was tucked back in a corner of the old church property, totally out of the wind, under that fiberglass awning.

But JD was so cold, felt like he might as well be lying outside on the sidewalk in his socks and underwear.

"Think this was a bad idea," Taylor said. "Should have gone to the shelter this afternoon, like I said." His voice came from the box beside JD.

JD didn't say anything, but secretly he agreed.

"You know it's going to get colder than this, few hours from now."

"I know," JD said, his teeth chattering. He reached for the whiskey bottle in his inside coat pocket. Took a quick swallow. Let the heat do its thing. "You got some whiskey?" he asked Taylor.

"I do. Don't think it's going to be enough."

"Still way better than Bastogne," JD said. "You know about Bastogne?"

"World War II."

"Right. Remember I told you about that article I read from that old *Look* magazine? That guy in there talked about how they spent a whole month in the freezing cold. A month, he said. No overcoat even. And no whiskey. And it wasn't just cold, they had snow, everywhere you looked."

"And people shooting at them," Taylor said. "And artillery shells exploding in the trees over their heads."

"That's right. So I think we can do this. One night, that's all we gotta make it."

"I hope you're right."

JD took another swig. Bottle felt pretty full, but he better pace it. Like Taylor said, couple of hours from now would be even worse. He remembered reading something else in that article he didn't mention to Taylor. Those guys in them foxholes buddied up together, real close, to stay warm. Like couples in love, the guy said, but quickly added there weren't no funny business. Guys just did what they had to do to stay warm.

In between whiskey swigs, JD felt almost cold enough to tell Taylor about that part. But he and Taylor, they didn't have that kind of relationship.

JD wasn't like that with anyone.

"Really, JD," Taylor said. "Think we made a bad call here."

17

Rick thought of one good thing to come out of this freezing weather: he'd sailed right over the bridge this morning. Way too cold for the sailboat owners to be out for a morning cruise. When he came out to his car, there had actually been frost on the windshield.

Still, nothing like winter mornings in Charlotte. But he'd forgotten how cold it could get down here. One of the river-front mansions had apparently left their sprinklers on. The whole backyard looked like a winter wonderland. Every tree and bush was frozen solid with silvery icicles shimmering in the sun. They even clung from the bottoms of low-hanging palms.

He drove through the old downtown area and pulled up in the parallel parking space beside the Book Nook. His was the only car on this side of the street. All morning, he'd been rehearsing what to say when he called his boss later today, asking to take the rest of the week off. They were expecting him back first thing tomorrow. Rick had worked at the firm for three years and felt pretty secure. His boss was actually a fairly nice guy to work for. But it was a large firm with lots of ambitious guys all looking to climb that proverbial ladder, by any means. If there wasn't enough room on the ladder, climbing on backs and necks would serve just as well.

This he knew firsthand.

As he stepped out from his car, a trail of vapor seeped through a manhole cover in the middle of the road. Thin layers of mist floated into the air from puddles along the edge of the street. He set his cup of Dunkin' Donuts coffee on the hood for a second. That's when he saw him peeking out from behind the corner of the church.

Columbo.

Only this time, he had a blanket wrapped around the overcoat, partially covering his head and shoulders, like some Arab warlord. The man backed away when he saw Rick.

Good idea, crazy man. Rick had no intention of acknowledging him this morning. If he wanted, he could come back at 3:00 when Andrea showed up. Rick got his things together and closed the car door. He carefully made his way down the little stairwell, almost slipping on a spot of ice clinging to one of the steps. He set his things on the concrete half-wall and fidgeted through his keys, looking for the one to the front door. He wasn't sure if it was the smell or the noise that alerted him, but he looked up and saw Columbo peeking around the corner again. Maybe five feet away.

He had better put a stop to this. "Hey," he called out. "You, around the corner." He couldn't remember the man's name. Some combination of initials.

The man stepped out in the open, then ducked back. Then stepped out completely. "You got it?" he asked.

"Got what?"

"It's almost 9:00. I been freezing all night. 'Bout the only thing keeping me goin' the past few hours was that it was almost 9:00."

"What are you talking about?"

"You don't got it?"

"Apparently not." Oh shoot, thought Rick. The Egg Mc-Muffin. "Look, you're going to have to go somewhere else for breakfast for a while."

"Where else?"

"I don't know. Where does everyone else go for breakfast, start there." Rick didn't want to look at the man's face. He didn't seem angry, more like confused.

"I'm so cold."

That will happen when you sleep outside, moron. "Well, so am I. Look, you come back in about twenty minutes, I'll give you a cup of coffee, but that's it. I'm not stopping off to get you Egg McMuffins. That was Art's thing, not mine."

"Twenty minutes?"

Great, Rick thought. Why did he say that? "Yeah, or there-abouts."

The man disappeared. Rick opened the door, then went back for his stuff and set it on the counter. He was about to head right back and start the coffee but decided, no, he wasn't going out of his way for this guy. He began going through the little startup routine Andrea had shown him.

Making coffee was step five.

Two hours later, the coffee in the Mr. Coffee maker was giving off a smell. Coffee was part of it, but something else had joined in. Rick wasn't used to this. The secretaries never let things get this far. Smelled like black licorice. At least it smelled and tasted right when he'd first made it; he and Columbo were the only ones who'd know. Not a single customer had come into the store yet.

The second ninety-minute Christmas cassette was playing through the store. At the moment, Johnny Cash sang "The Little Drummer Boy." He lifted the coffeepot out. The smell was much stronger now and the coffee two shades darker. Should he make a full pot or a half pot?

Such decisions.

A few days ago, he'd helped an owner of a multimillion-dollar lumber company decide if he had sufficient capital to buy out a competitor who'd fallen on hard times.

Rick walked the carafe back to the sink, holding it out like a stinky diaper. As he fixed the next pot, he heard voices over his shoulder. Elderly ladies. Must have come in while the water was running. He turned to see them. They were by the greeting cards two aisles over. All he could see were the tops of their hairdos, both curly, one silver, the other darker.

He sighed when he recognized their voices. Molly and Fran, if he remembered right. They reminded him of Lucy and Ethel from *I Love Lucy*, if the show had gone on another twenty years. He probably should acknowledge them in some way. He pushed the start button and walked over but stopped one aisle back and listened to their conversation.

"Molly, how come none of these cards say 'Good Luck' or 'Best Wishes'?"

"What?"

"Can't find a single card that says 'Good Luck on Your Birthday.' Birthday cards always say that . . . or 'Best Wishes.'"

"We don't believe in luck or sending wishes."

"We don't?"

"Not anymore. We're Christians, Fran. Christians don't believe in such things."

"We don't? I've been sending cards all my life wishing people good luck. What's the harm?"

"No harm, it's just . . . well, it's just stupid."

"Good luck is stupid?"

"Think about it, dear. You think there's some big luck dispenser in the sky? What . . . some luck angel or luck elf fills up a glass and sprinkles it over people they like?"

"I suppose it is rather silly," Fran said. "But I've had bad luck all my life. You know that. You always say, 'You're the unluckiest person I know.'"

"Well, I don't say it anymore."

"No, I suppose you don't. So what do you figure happened to all my bad luck then?"

"Nothing happened. Your bad luck never happened. You want me to say it? Okay, I was wrong. You're not the unluckiest person I know."

"Really?"

"Yes. Now, please, can we just pick out a card?"

"Okay, but most of these are red and green. They look more like Christmas cards."

"That's because they are, dear. Come over to this rack."

"Oh," said Fran. They quietly worked their way through the cards. Then Fran said, "The thing is . . . I've always believed I *was* unlucky. It kinda made sense. I don't know what I'm supposed to think now."

"Are you still harping on that?" said Molly. "Now, see, whatever it was you had, it wasn't bad luck. And it's all in the past now, washed by the blood."

"Amen, sister," said Fran. She paused a moment, then got the biggest smile.

Rick, standing one aisle back, just shook his head.

Who are these people?

18

Rick thought better of interrupting the two sisters with some pretentious greeting, so he walked down the aisle, got behind the counter. Made just enough noise so they'd know he was there. He looked through a small stack of LPs, the records Andrea had used to make up the ninety-minute cassettes playing through the store. She'd said folks would often come up and ask who was singing this or that song. Then they'd go right over and buy the album.

Except for a few big names from the real world—like Johnny Cash or BJ Thomas—Rick hadn't heard of a single one. He was reading the back of an album cover when Molly came up to greet him.

She set a birthday card on the counter. "It's Rick, right?"

"Yes. Will that be all for you today?" He hoped a courteous, professional demeanor might forestall any chitchat.

"This'll be it for me, but Fran back there . . . she's feeling guilty about just buying Madeline a card. Me? I don't think Madeline will mind. Now, I will buy her a Christmas present in a couple of weeks." She leaned across the counter as if to whisper, but it still came out pretty loud. "Truth is, Fran'll feel guilty with just one of us giving Madeline a birthday present. She'll write on the gift tag that it's from both of us, so I come out ahead either way."

Rick forced a smile. "Want me to ring this up, or do you want to wait for her and pay together?"

"Heavens no, ring it up. She's got her money, I've got mine."

He rang it up, told her the price. She handed him a five, and he gave her change. Rick put the card in a bag and handed it to Molly. She was staring at him.

"Trying to see whether you look more like Leanne or Art," she said.

"It would have to be Leanne. Art's not my father."

"You don't say. Well, that was going to be my guess anyways. Could have come from either one, though, and you'd have turned out fine. Best folks I ever met, Art and Leanne. Changed our lives for good a year back." She leaned forward and loud-whispered, "Especially for Fran there."

Molly was about to unload on him. He could feel it. He was trapped.

"See, we'd come in here off and on, like today, and get a gift for someone. Most of our friends are churchgoers. But we'd been going to a church all our lives that never explained anything. Very traditional. Guess they figured they taught us all we needed as kids. Anyway, we believed in God, even believed in Jesus, but poor Fran here was so unhappy. All the time. Never smiled. Lived all alone till my poor Bill died a few years ago, then she moved in with me."

Please . . . someone come through that door. Someone call on the phone.

"I knew what it was made her so unhappy. But she'd never talk to me." Molly leaned forward again. "Happened during World War II. She was in love with a guy named Hank. She wanted them to get married. He wanted to wait till he got back from the war. But a few nights before he shipped out, they got a little too close, if you get my meaning."

Why was she telling him this? No wonder Fran didn't talk to her.

"Poor ol' Hank got himself killed at Iwo Jima, and Fran was sure God was punishing her for what they'd done. And because of it, she never married, though she had plenty of takers. She lived under the guilt of that thing right up until one of our visits here to the Book Nook a year back."

Rick looked over at Fran. How long can a woman take to pick out the right knickknack?

"We'd come in here, and each time your folks treated us so nice. Your mom especially took an interest in Fran. Like she could see the hurt in her eyes. She took it real slow, asked Fran some questions, never too personal. Served us that delicious coffee. Sometimes with muffins. And there was always this beautiful music playing. After a few visits, I could see Fran warming up to her."

Rick had a thought. "Speaking of coffee, I just made a fresh pot. Care for a cup?"

"Maybe when Fran gets up here. Anyway, one of those visits—I'll remember this day as long as I live—we had just sat down for coffee. Art was up front here watching the counter. Nobody in the store but us. Next thing I know, Fran is telling Leanne all these deep things she's lived with all these years, crying up a storm. Then I start crying. Leanne just sits there calmly, holding Fran's hand, helping her get it all out till Fran had nothing left to say."

Molly's eyes were tearing up as she spoke. Rick saw a box of tissues next to the register and slid it over.

"Then Leanne opened up a Bible on the coffee table, read a few verses to Fran, and explained what they meant. She said, 'Fran, you see what this is saying? God doesn't want you living your whole life carrying all that guilt over your sin. That's why he sent Jesus. He punished Jesus for what we've done. That's what the gospel's all about. Us putting faith in what he did for us on the cross. God doesn't hate you, Fran. He loves you . . . right this very minute and for the rest of your life.'"

Molly picked up a tissue and dabbed her eyes. Just about then, Fran came walking up full of smiles. She noticed Molly with the tissues. "Now, what in the world?"

"I'm just telling Rick here about that day his mama changed our lives."

"Figured it had to be something to get you in such a state." She set her card and two Precious Moments figurines on the counter. "Both your mom and your dad are—"

"Art's not his daddy," Molly said. "He's your stepdad, right?"

Rick nodded.

"Well, as I was saying, Art and Leanne are the dearest couple we've ever known. Molly and I were just saying that yesterday over morning coffee."

"And we meant it," Molly added. "Then we said a prayer for Art. A long one."

Fran looked Rick straight in the eye and said, "It's wonderful meeting you, Rick. But I gotta tell you, it's hard not to think of Art standing there behind that counter." She reached for a tissue.

"Oh, stop now, Fran. I just got cleaned up. Now you got me going again." Molly reached for a tissue.

Rick felt nothing, except a strong hope that this visit was about to wrap up. Felt if he said a single warm or friendly thing, it would never stop. "So will this be all for you?"

"Yes, but I need to explain something." Fran held up one of the figurines. "This one, I'll take with me. But this one . . ." She held up another, looked like a little Indian or an angel. "I'd like you to give this to your mom from me. Well, say it's from Molly and me."

Rick looked at Molly, who winked at him behind Fran's back.

Fran turned it over. "Make sure she sees what it says on the bottom. See? 'His Burden Is Light.'"

Rick rang everything up and said, "Have a nice day. I'll make sure my mom gets this. I'm sure she'll love it." They both patted Rick on the hand as they turned to leave. He felt sure they wanted to exchange hugs. But he stood still and they started for the door.

Molly led the way. As she turned the doorknob, she stopped and said, "Good heavens, Fran. I almost forgot, while you were shopping Rick asked if we'd like to stay for coffee."

19

Thankfully, Rick's coffee break with Molly and Fran had been cut short by a rush of lunchtime customers. Thinking on it now, he had to admit the ladies were as sweet as they were odd, and he was grateful they didn't require any help from him to keep the conversation flowing. He had sat through one almost-childish spat, after Fran insisted Molly had a crush on Ronald Reagan, the new president. Molly flatly denied it.

Most of the time had been spent talking about who shot JR, which had been revealed on *Dallas* last week. They couldn't fathom how anyone in the civilized world could have missed such an historic moment. Fran said that episode had the highest ratings of any television show in history. It said so in *TV Guide*.

Wasn't that something.

Rick looked around. The store was empty again. A Christmas cassette played through the store. Mr. Coffee was slowly brewing a fresh pot of coffee in the back. Rick ate a second slice of banana nut bread one of the customers had left. She'd asked him to bring it to his mother at the hospital. But it was after 1:00 p.m. and he'd forgotten his lunch. He knew his mom believed in sharing.

Rick stared at the telephone. Before he lost the nerve, he picked it up, dialed the number, and gave a brief summary to his boss's secretary. She quickly put him through.

"Rick, how's it going, my man? How'd your skiing trip go? Was it Aspen this time?"

His boss was in a good mood; his lunch appointment must have gone his way. "I'm doing fine, Mr. Rainey, but . . . well, things didn't turn out the way I planned. Hope you had a nice Thanksgiving."

"Food was good, company was tolerable. This year it was my wife's family's turn, so we were down in Mobile. So . . . what happened to you?"

Rick filled him in about Art and how that had abruptly changed Rick's holiday plans. "The thing is now . . . the doctors are saying he needs surgery, but his brain is still too swollen to operate."

"So you're going to have to stay down there another, what, two or three days?"

"Actually, I'm going to need to stay at least the rest of the week."

"Really?"

Rick didn't like the tone in that reply. "I'm sorry to spring this on you, sir. But I don't see any other way. It's a small store, but it's their whole livelihood, and she doesn't have anyone else who can fill in. You know how retail is the weeks just after Thanksgiving. It's their highest sales volume."

"But . . . it is just a retail job, right? Can't they call a temp service?"

"I checked. Town's too small. They don't even have one."

"Well, it's your vacation time, Rick. You know our policy. It's yours to use as you please, long as our clients' needs come first. I'm assuming you had a pretty full schedule set for this week. We're heading into year's end, things heat up pretty—"

"I know, Mr. Rainey." Rick sighed. "It's a terrible time for this to happen."

"Just thinking of you, Rick. I'll take a look at your appointments this week, see who can fill in."

"Actually, sir, I've already figured something out. I was going to call my secretary next and see how many appointments I can bump till next week. For those who can't, I'll call other associates to support them, see if they can keep the plates spinning till I get back." If Rick had to get anyone else involved with his clients, he wanted to pick them.

"That's good, Rick. You already thought it through then. Well, do what you have to do down there. We'll see you back here next week."

"Thanks, Mr. Rainey."

"Don't come back with too much of a tan," he said. "Folks might doubt your cover story."

"Right, sir." Rick hung up.

He hadn't solved his problem, just bought himself a little time. Rick knew Art wouldn't be up and about by next week. Not with open-cranial surgery. He'd be down at least this week and the next.

If he survived at all.

After the lunchtime rush, things quieted down again. He looked at his watch. Andrea should be coming in an hour or two from now. Seemed like a safe time to head back to Art's office and do some paperwork. Maybe telephone the vendors on Andrea's reorder list.

He looked up at the front door and made a mental note to buy some kind of bell, something to let him know when people came in. He stopped at the cassette player, turned the volume down, then walked to the office, stood in the doorway.

Really, this wasn't an office.

It was barely bigger than a broom closet. The desktop was an interior door, cut in half and wedged in a corner. The other end rested on a rusty two-drawer file cabinet. In the middle sat a swivel chair that didn't swivel, the back wrapped in duct tape to keep a rip from getting worse. Paint was chipping off one wall. The paneling on the other was warped and pulling away. Nothing matched. Rick sat down and slid the reorder sheet from the inbox.

For the next thirty minutes, he called each of the vendors on the list. It was a humiliating experience. Half the vendors turned him down. All for the same reason. *"I'm sorry. We can't send you any new inventory until we receive payment for orders already received."*

"How much do you need before you can process the order?" he'd asked. He wrote the various amounts down on a separate sheet of paper, then totaled it up.

Just over eight hundred dollars.

Didn't seem like much at first. Pocket change back in Charlotte. Rick searched around and found the store's checkbook. He flipped to the last check stub to see how much money they had in the bank. He couldn't believe it; there was no balance. He turned back through pages of stubs to find the last time a balance had been recorded. Over three weeks ago. And there were all kinds of handwritten notes scribbled in the margin, arrows drawn here and there, referencing one check number or another. Several times, balances had been crossed out and new figures written in above them.

He reached for Art's bookkeeping journal and opened it, hoping it might shed some light. It was even worse. Looking at it more closely, he knew one thing for sure: Art routinely operated with a negative balance. There was almost as much red ink as black, and the last eight balance entries were red.

The whole thing was a mess.

He looked up from the desk. This office was a dump. The

store was a dump. Art's books were trash. This was no way to run a business. Rick hated to add to his mom's stress, but he needed to call her and make her aware of this, get her permission to sort this all out.

It was that bad.

20

Leanne was almost getting used to the new routine. Wake up stiff and sore, both back and hips. Glance at Art, then his numbers. Fold up the sheets and blanket, put the chair-bed back together. Glance at Art, then his numbers. Brush down the parts of her hair that stuck out the worst, try not to look at her face in the mirror while doing so. Look back at Art through the mirror. Brush her teeth. Walk over and kiss Art on the forehead. Carry her bag, robe, and towel to the room they provided nearby for a shower. And as quickly as possible, try to make herself presentable in case Art woke up.

After the morning routine, she'd come back to sit, pray, and read for most of the day. Every so often, look up at Art and pray some more. Oh yes, eat hospital food three times a day. Breakfast this morning had been a poached egg, dry toast, and a banana. For lunch: macaroni and cheese, vanilla pudding. It wasn't so bad, not like everyone says. More than anything, she missed her coffee. They had coffee here, but it was awful. Art always said hers was the best.

She looked up at Art, checked his numbers again. His vital signs had remained stable today, and that was a good thing. Dr. Halper seemed pleased. He'd been in just after lunch and said the swelling in Art's brain was decreasing some.

Another day or two and he felt Art might be strong enough to move to Shands.

This was the only upside in Leanne's life at the moment.

She felt so lonely. Mostly for Art. The desire to talk with him gnawed inside her like hunger pangs. She also missed Andrea and little Amy, especially now; Amy was so delightful to be with at Christmastime. And Leanne missed all the customers who filled her days with so much conversation and adventure.

She was glad for one thing: the Lord did seem close to her, even closer than usual. But she could only grab a few precious moments alone here and there. The hospital staff was treating her so well, but with these big glass partitions, it felt like living in an aquarium.

Something caught her eye. She looked up; a nurse waved at her through the glass. She made a hand signal suggesting she had a phone call. Leanne looked at Art then set her book on the chair and hurried to the doorway.

"You have a phone call in the waiting room. Your son, Rick."

"Thank you." Rick didn't call often. She hoped everything was okay. She walked quickly to the waiting room, glad to find it empty. "Hi, Rick. How's it going, your first day on your own?"

"Pretty smooth. It was a little slow in the morning, but very steady during lunch. Those ladies came in again, Molly and Fran."

Leanne smiled, imagining the scene. "They are quite a pair."

"They brought me up to speed on *Dallas*."

"Did they?"

"Did you know someone shot JR?"

Leanne laughed. "I'd heard something about that."

"Yeah, well . . . guess I better get to why I called. I had

some time before Andrea comes in, thought I'd reorder some things today, hoping they might get here by the weekend."

"Thanks for doing that. Did you find everything you need? I know Art's got his own system. I've never understood it."

"Well, that's the thing. I ran into some snags. One pretty big one."

"What's the matter?" She sighed. She knew so little about how Art handled the paperwork.

"Did Art say anything to you about how much money the store has in the bank?"

"I don't . . . well, I know we pay everything but the book vendors on time. He has some kind of system worked out about when to pay them. Why, what's the problem?"

Rick spent the next five minutes explaining the mess he'd found trying to make sense of Art's "system." Her stomach was starting to turn. She didn't need this right now. "What can we do?"

"I'm pretty good at this, Mom. If you'll trust me, I think I can dig out of this, then let you know where things are at."

"Oh, Rick." She was tearing up. "Of course, I trust you. Do whatever you have to."

"What about when Art wakes up? He might not like me messing with his system."

"Don't worry. I'm going to do everything I can to keep his mind off anything like that. If you can make sense of it, and get to where you can write checks to the vendors, go right ahead and I'll sign them."

"All right, I'll see what I can do."

———————▲———————

Rick had been staring at the ledger, trying to decipher Art's riddles for over an hour. A headache had started to form in his temples and behind his eyes. He heard Andrea come in. He got up, glad for the distraction. The Christmas music had shut off at some point, so he quickly hit the play button as he walked by. "Afternoon," he said.

She set her purse on the counter and took off her heavy coat. She had her hair pulled back like the first day, with barrettes. She wore a thick white sweater over blue jeans. Rick thought he saw some makeup around her eyes, and her cheeks were a little redder. He flattered himself that this might be for his sake. "How's your first day going?" she asked.

"Slow morning, very busy at lunch. Just a handful coming in between now and then." He walked up to the front side of the counter. Felt a little like being at a bar. "I'll have a White Russian," he said.

"What?"

He shook his head. "Bad joke." She seemed to think a moment, then nodded as if she got it. "Those two sisters came in."

"Molly and Fran?"

Rick nodded. "So, I need to ask you . . . did you figure out who shot JR?"

Andrea laughed. "Actually . . . I couldn't care less. Never watch the show. Comes on too late."

"Too late?"

"Television's in the room Amy sleeps in. What else they talk about?"

Rick spent a few minutes filling her in. "Something else came up after lunch, something pretty serious." He explained what happened when he'd called the vendors on her reorder list, then what he'd discovered wading through Art's bookkeeping system. It was hard to hide his frustration over the mess Art had made of things. But he did his best, knowing how Andrea felt about Art.

"I'm not shocked," Andrea said. "Art is the sweetest, kindest man I ever met, but he's never struck me as a shrewd businessman. For one thing, he gives too many things away."

"What do you mean? What's he give away?"

"I wouldn't be surprised if Art's read every book in here. People will come in, he'll go up and talk with them. They'll ask him for advice. I mean, they'll just open right up and pour their hearts out. That part I get. He's so easy to talk to. Like your mom, he just listens so well, asks questions. Then he'll pick out a couple of books that would be perfect for what they're going through. They won't know which one to pick, so he'll tell them to have a seat on the couch, and he'll fix them a cup of coffee. He'll say, 'Look 'em over. Take your time. Pick out the one that's the best fit.'" Andrea walked over to the heater and put her hands out.

"I don't know how many times they'd put one back, come up to the counter with the other. He'd see it and ask them why they picked that one. They'd say they couldn't afford both. You know what he'd do?"

Rick shook his head no, but he knew.

"While I rang up the book they picked, he'd go over, grab the one they put back, and put it in their bag. 'I think the Lord wants you to have this one too,' he'd say." She smiled. "He's so generous and caring."

Rick wasn't smiling. He had a different thought.

I think the Lord wants you to pay your bills.

21

Rick was sitting in what had now become "his" booth at HoJo's, eating what had now become "the usual" for breakfast. He thought about the rest of yesterday afternoon at the Book Nook. Went by fast. Time always flew by when he was working on a tough accounting problem. Andrea had kept watch at the counter, freeing him to stay in the back office. The one bright spot in the day was when she came back, handing him one of the best cups of coffee he'd ever had.

Then he wondered, was it the coffee or the fact that he had just been wishing for a cup when she showed up—or that she brought it on her own without asking? He liked that. Maybe it was just the dramatic contrast to the horrible excuse for coffee in his cup right now.

After they locked up, he'd dropped by the hospital to get his mom's signature on the deposit slip. He had just over twenty-one hundred to deposit, mostly cash. Certainly seemed enough to cover the eight hundred dollars of reorders, so he'd brought the checks made out to those vendors with him also.

He forced the last sip of coffee down. He was running late this morning, as usual. Last night he'd forgotten to ask his mom where their bank was.

"Want a refill on that?"

Rick looked up. "No thanks, Sally. I've got to go."

"Want to take some in a to-go cup?"

"That's all right. I usually just drink one cup in the morning."

"I'll have your check up by the counter."

He looked at his watch. Not enough time to swing by Dunkin' Donuts. Now *that* would be some good coffee. But hey, he could make a decent cup now. He got up and walked to the register. "Say, Sally, know where the nearest Barnett Bank is?"

She thought a moment. "Used to be one downtown, but I think they closed that branch. There's one close to the new mall they're building out by the highway, on one of the main corners."

"Thanks." He paid the bill, went back to the table, and left her a nice tip. Wouldn't be time to drive out to the bank and open the store on time. It could wait till after the lunch rush; he'd bring the deposit by then.

He headed over to the store, surprised he didn't even need a jacket. It had warmed up that much. As he pulled up, he was glad Columbo was nowhere in sight. He opened up, went through the routine Andrea had taught him. Only today he moved making the coffee to the front of the checklist.

Things went fairly smoothly for the next two hours. Just a steady stream of fairly normal customers who, thankfully, didn't ask too many questions. Then around 11:30 a.m., two long-haired guys walked in, about college age. One carried a guitar case. Rick thought his own hair had been at least that long back in high school. These guys were both blond. Clearly surfer types, wearing baggies, surfer shirts, and flip-flops.

The one carrying the guitar looked startled when he saw Rick. Then he got this big smile. "Hey, bro," he said to his friend, "take this and head back to the sofa I told you about.

They got the best coffee in here, and it's free." He walked over to Rick. "Hey, dude, where's Art and Leanne?"

"I'm Leanne's son, Rick."

"For real? Love your folks. They're far out. I'm Mack. Not my first name. Last name's McAdams. But you can call me Mack."

Rick explained Art's situation to Mack, using the simplest words possible. Mack's face grew more and more concerned as he listened. "Man, that's so sad," he said. "I'll get my folks prayin' for him. Art's like the coolest old dude I ever met."

"Thanks," Rick said. "Anything I can help you with?"

"No, just brought my friend James in. Our class at the junior college got cancelled, got some time to kill. Thought we'd come in and check out some tunes."

He couldn't mean this Christmas music.

Mack started walking back toward his friend, then stopped. "If I went to the hospital, would they let me see him?"

"Sorry. He's in ICU, no visitors."

"Bummer." Mack shook his head. "It was Art who first turned me on to these tunes. I got saved at this youth rally last year. Thought I'd have to start listening to choir music for the rest of my life till I came here. Art told me all about these guys, good as anything out there, he said. I'm thinking, you're just an old dude, what could you know. He opened up three cassettes right there on the spot: Phil Keaggy, 2nd Chapter of Acts, Randy Stonehill. I'm listening, thinking, no way this is Christian."

Rick smiled dumbly. He had no idea who these people were.

"Well, you tell Leanne that Mack says hi. And tell her . . . keep looking up."

"I will."

Mack continued toward the back of the store but stopped at the record section. "Dude, no way," he yelled. "James, come here. The Pat Terry Group's new album is out. They're the group I was telling you about. Remember? The ones that sound like Crosby, Stills, Nash and Young?"

"I remember," James said, getting up from the sofa.

"C'mere, James. Check it out."

Rick thought he heard a crackling sound, like cellophane tearing. What were they doing?

"Too bad they only have one set of headphones," James said.

"Not a problem," Mack said. "Nobody's in the store. Here."

Rick heard a click; the Christmas music stopped playing. What the heck? He came out from behind the counter. A few seconds later, a nice rhythm guitar sound started playing through the speakers. Then a fairly pleasant male voice began singing, soon joined by another voice singing in perfect harmony. Did sound a little like Crosby, Stills, Nash and Young. But that wasn't the point. Rick stood at the front of the aisle, hands on his hips, eyeing the two young men.

Both were looking at the record rack, nodding their heads to the beat of the song. Mack caught a glimpse of Rick and turned toward him. "Dude, you ever heard these guys?"

"What are you doing?"

"Pat Terry. I love these guys." He was smiling from ear to ear.

Rick saw the cellophane wrapper lying on top of some albums. Mack had ripped open the cassette. "You plan on paying for that?"

Still nodding to the beat and smiling, Mack said, "Maybe."

Rick took a few steps in their direction. "I think you are . . . *dude*."

"Hey, dude, don't get all uptight. It's cool. Art lets us do this."

"He what?"

"He said sometimes they send free copies of the new stuff

as demos. When they don't, he said we can open up one to check it out, see if we like it before plopping down the cash. I'd never do something like this if Art wasn't cool with it."

That was nice. At least Art was cool with it.

"Look," Mack said, pointing to a small box full of cassettes. "See? All these are demos. Art said it's good for business."

Rick sighed.

"Usually I just use the headphones," Mack said. "But then James couldn't hear it. You're cool with me turning off 'Jingle Bells' for a few minutes, right? I'll put it back in when we're done, or if anyone else comes in the store. You know, like old folks."

What else could Rick say? "I guess if it's okay with Art."

"Cool."

That Art, Rick thought, he knows what's good for business.

22

Mack and his surfer buddy had left once the lunchtime shoppers started coming in. He'd vowed to be back later. "Once I snatch some cash from my stash back home." He said it was to buy the Pat Terry Group cassette he'd opened up.

It was about 1:30 now. The last of the lunch hour shoppers had just left. The store was quiet again, except for the Jingle Bell music, as Mack called it.

Mack had stirred up some old memories for Rick. For starters, he remembered how much he used to envy surfers. They were the coolest bunch in high school. Got invited to the best parties, had the best-looking girlfriends. Rick wanted to be one, but after his mom married Art, they moved into Art's house on the mainland, far away from the beach. Too far for a kid without a car.

Art had kept inviting Rick to go out fishing with him. That's what he was into. Rick could tell it was Art's way of trying to get them to spend time together, become more like a father and son. But that wasn't going to happen. It went on for months. Rick remembered one Saturday morning when he finally had to tell Art to just back off on this father thing.

Rick was in bed, trying to sleep in. Art came into his room. Rick opened his eyes but didn't move. Art was all dressed to go out fishing again, holding a tackle box and two poles. "Say, Rick," he said, a little louder than a whisper. "Heading out this morning. A friend told me the snook are really biting out there. Wanna come? I'll have you back in a couple of hours. You'd still have the whole day to yourself."

Rick ignored him.

"What do you think?" Art asked again.

"Art, would you just stop this?" Rick said. "I'm not going fishing with you." He rolled over and faced the wall. "You don't think I get what you're trying to do? Just give it up. You're not my father. You're never going to be my father. I didn't ask you to marry my mom. Okay?"

Art didn't say anything. Rick waited. Heard Art's footsteps fading away. The door closing.

Art seemed to get the message after that. Rick felt bad—for two seconds. It had to be said. Art was nothing like Rick's father. If Rick's father had still been around, he'd have found a way to help Rick become a surfer. He probably would have been right out there in the ocean with him. His dad loved to have fun.

Even back then, Art had seemed old to him. Rick didn't want to go out fishing with "some old dude." Didn't want to spend his free time taking in the quiet Florida scenery and listening to Art's lectures about life.

That was about the time Rick pulled away from the little "family unit." He'd drifted into the long-haired druggie group at school. The party-hardy, rock-and-roll crowd. He'd always gotten straight As before this and somehow managed to keep enough brain cells alive to land a full scholarship based on his GPA. He'd worked part-time his junior and senior year, bought his VW van, and headed off to college two months after graduating high school.

He never did go fishing with Art, and he never learned how to surf.

Rick was thinking about these things as he locked the front door to the Book Nook. Once again, he'd forgotten to bring anything for lunch, and he was starving. Got an idea to drive around the corner to Beach Street, get something at the diner where Andrea worked. He taped a little sign inside the door: "Back in 1 hour."

It was a bright, sunny day, felt like about seventy degrees outside. The kind of winter day that gets so many people up north to move down here. Rick hopped in his Celica and drove off. He pushed in that Pat Terry cassette Mack had been playing. He actually wanted to hear some more. A few minutes later, he was driving slowly down Beach Street, looking for the Driftwood Diner.

It was a shame to see so many stores closed up, especially since he could remember what it had looked like when he was a kid. Sears sat at one end of Beach Street, JCPenney's at the other, with all the smaller stores and restaurants in between. The two big stores were still there but had big signs in the windows: Moving Soon to the New Mall!

There was the diner, with a closed-down shoe repair shop on one side, a closed jewelry store on the other. Rick pulled into one of the many parking spaces available. Before turning the car off, he sat there, puzzled at the sentimental feelings going on inside him.

Why should he care what happened to these stores on Beach Street? Just a few days ago, he'd seen this same scene and thought it a good thing, evidence of economic progress.

He got out of the car and stepped over the curb. Didn't see Andrea yet. The Driftwood Diner had a half dozen tables outside under an awning. All empty. He walked through the glass door and saw her bringing drinks to two elderly women at the end of a row of more empty tables. For a moment, he was about to turn right around and head back out the door but then realized it wasn't Molly and Fran.

The diner had a fifties look to it, black and white tile, red and white checkerboard tablecloths, an old soda fountain bar wrapping around the right side with swiveling padded stools. As he looked closer, he realized it wasn't a decorating style. This stuff looked like it might be original.

Andrea turned and saw him, smiled and waved. She really looked cute in her little getup and apron. Like the kind of waitress guys couldn't help but hit on. He found himself a little edgy at that thought as he smiled and nodded.

"Just pick a seat anywhere," she said as she walked an empty tray around the counter. "I'll be right over."

Rick picked a booth near the window, grabbed a menu from a metal clip near the wall. It was simple lunchtime fare. Burgers, dogs, fries, chili, sodas, and milk shakes, fixed just the way you like 'em.

"Who's watching the store?" she asked.

He looked up to find her standing right there. "Nobody. Seems like it empties out about now for an hour or so. Did yesterday, same thing today. Forgot my lunch, so I thought I'd pop in here and get something. What's good and fast?" he asked.

"It's all fast," she said, smiling. "Guess the cheeseburger's what everybody gets. Kinda greasy, but I think that's on purpose."

"Then I'll have that, extra grease, fries, and a Coke."

"You want cherry in the Coke?"

"Sure, extra cherry."

She laughed and was about to walk away.

"Can you visit a little after you put in the order?" Rick said.

She looked over her shoulder. "Not really. The owner's got a rule about that, even if the restaurant's completely empty, he doesn't want the help sitting down."

"That's all right. I really should just wolf down lunch and head back."

"Let me go put this in then. I can stand over here for a few minutes, after I stop by my other table."

He watched her head back toward the kitchen, through a swinging door. A few minutes later she came out with a tray full of food and dropped it off to the women at the end. She glanced once more at the kitchen door then headed toward Rick.

"How do you guys stay open?" he asked quietly. "How do you survive on tips with no customers?"

"It's not bad, actually. We were hopping around here thirty minutes ago. Same at breakfast. It completely drops off in between."

"Really? Where do these customers come from? Looks pretty dead out there." He pointed toward the street with his eyes.

"This place couldn't make it," she said, leaning forward, "except there's a few big law firms down by Sears and then the courthouse by the Silver Street bridge. Thankfully, they're not going anywhere once the mall opens, so we should be okay. Let me get your cherry Coke."

A few moments later, she came back with it. He took a sip, ice cold, really tasted good. "See, I knew you'd like the cherry," Andrea said. "I'll go check on your burger."

"Think it will be done already?"

"He's pretty quick with this stuff."

Rick thought it was just as well. He really didn't want to be gone too long. Besides, he had to drive out to the bank and make that—shoot! He just realized . . . he left the bank envelope at the store, under the counter.

"What's wrong?" she said, setting the burger and fries down in front of him.

"Nothing. I just realized I've got to swing by the store after here. Remember that bank deposit I put together yesterday? Had to go by the hospital last night, get my mom's signature on a check for petty cash. The bank was closed by then."

"If you want, as dead as it is in here, I'll probably get off right at 2:30. You could wait on the bank till then, and I'll watch the store while you go."

"No, that's all right." He picked up a couple of fries. "I'll just do it now. Don't want to take a chance we get too busy and I miss getting the money in there again before it closes."

She smiled. "I've gotta go check on my ladies. Everything okay here?"

"Nice and greasy, just like I ordered." He looked to the left by the wall. "And there's the ketchup. Looks like I'm all set."

"Let me know if you need anything," she said as she walked down the row of tables toward the two women.

He picked up his burger and took a bite. It was greasy and crispy. The buns were basted in butter and grilled also. Simply delicious.

As he took the next bite, he found himself staring at Andrea. She really was . . . beautiful. Instantly he knew his real reason for rejecting her offer to go to the bank while she waited at the store. It had nothing to do with worrying about the bank being closed. It was about cutting into the time he'd get to spend with her at the store.

For that matter, he knew why he'd really come here for lunch in the first place. He took a sip of cherry Coke.

What are you thinking? She's got a kid.

⸻

Standing by the counter, Andrea waved to Rick as he left the diner. It was empty now. She grabbed a washcloth and an empty gray tub, intending to clean up his table. She set both down and quickly walked to the window, standing back several feet until she saw his car begin to pull away. As it did, she took a few steps closer and watched it head down Beach Street.

"That the guy?"

It was Sal, her boss.

"What?" she said. She hurried over to Rick's table, began gathering things into the tub.

"The guy who was just here," he said, walking down the counter aisle.

She glanced up at him standing there in his white apron and T-shirt, a towel slung over his shoulder. "What do you mean?" She knew what he meant.

"The guy. You know, the guy you been talking about the last few days. Art and Leanne's boy."

Had she been talking about Rick? She must have, for Sal to ask. "He's not Art and Leanne's boy, just Leanne's. Art's his stepfather."

"Guess it's him then. So what, something happenin' between you two?"

"What?" she said, wiping the table down. "No, there's nothing—why would you even say that, Sal?"

"I was lookin', saw the way he was lookin' at you. The way most the guys who come in here look at you. Thing is . . . I never seen you follow them out and watch them drive away."

This was horrible. She was so embarrassed. "I wasn't following him out. I was just—"

"C'mon, Andrea. You gonna tell me you suddenly got interested in nice cars? Hey, relax. It's no big deal. You know I been saying you need to get out more, start having a social life." He started walking back to the kitchen, then stopped. "And Amy . . . I bet you ask her, she might like to have a daddy someday."

"Sal!"

"What?"

"Now you've got me married off to this guy? There's

nothing going on between us. I just met him a few days ago. And I can already tell, we've got nothing in common."

He turned toward the kitchen door. Just before he walked through the swinging door, he said over his shoulder, "My mama used to say something about opposites."

23

Rick drove the few city blocks back to the store. From one block away he looked up, glad to see there wasn't a crowd waiting out front. Just one high-school-aged kid standing on the sidewalk, holding a skateboard. As Rick got close to the church, something seemed wrong.

The kid was looking around nervously at the store's front door, then down the street, then back at the door. Rick was so focused on the kid, he didn't even notice the front door. The kid turned as Rick's car stopped. He was saying something and pointing toward the door. Rick looked at it as he got out of the car. It was standing wide open, and the glass panel nearest the doorknob was shattered.

The bank deposit!

"No, no, no," Rick muttered as he ran around the car. "Kid, what happened? Is there someone in there now?"

"No," the kid said. "I was skating on the sidewalk by the front of the church. When I got to the corner there, I heard some guy crying out in pain. He was coming up those steps fast, but I guess he tripped."

"Where is he?" Rick asked, walking down the steps.

"He took off running, that way." He pointed south. "On the sidewalk. He was limping. At that first block, he crossed the street and kept running."

"Stay here a minute, will you?" Rick ran inside. The cash register drawer was wide open. And it was empty. He ran past it and reached under the counter. The deposit bag was gone. Over two thousand dollars. He ran back out front; the kid was getting ready to skate away. "Hey, kid, wait!"

"I don't want to get messed up in this. I gotta get home."

"C'mon, kid . . . what's your name?"

"Jed."

"Okay, Jed. Look, you're the only one saw this guy. Can you tell me what he looked like?"

"Some homeless guy, looked like it anyway."

"Can you describe him?"

"I don't know . . . homeless. Had a big old coat on, hair all over the place, scraggly beard."

Columbo, Rick thought. "I'm gonna call the cops," he said. "They'll want to talk to you."

"Sorry, man, I'm outta here." He skated across the intersection.

"Hold on . . . Jed, stop." But he kept going. A few seconds later he was out of sight. Rick ran back in the store and dialed 911.

"911, what's the nature of your emergency?"

"A robbery, a break-in, at St. Luke's Church downtown. Actually, the little bookstore on the corner."

"Are you there now, sir?"

"Yes, it just happened, maybe five, ten minutes ago. He couldn't have gone far. Please send someone immediately."

"Did you see the suspect?"

"No, a high school kid was here when I got here, but he left."

"Do you think he's the suspect?"

"No, he told me it was a homeless guy. The kid didn't have anything on him, just a skateboard. But, look, this guy stole everything in the cash drawer and a bank deposit, with over two thousand dollars cash." Rick sighed loudly. "I can't believe this."

"A patrolman is on his way, sir. He's only a few blocks from you. Can you stay on the line?"

"Yes, well . . . yes. But I think I know who did this."

"Can you describe him?"

"I didn't actually see him, but there's this homeless guy been hanging around the store the last few days. I chased him off. He matches the description the kid gave me."

"Can you describe him?"

"Older guy, wearing a big overcoat, lots of hair, dark hair, scraggly beard."

The dispatcher repeated back what he said.

"Well, I guess the kid didn't say dark hair. Maybe he did. I don't remember. But there's another thing. The guy might have a good bruise on his shin or somewhere on his leg. The kid said he tripped as he ran up the stairs, hard enough that he yelled out in pain."

"All right, sir, Sergeant West should be arriving any moment. He says he has the church in sight. Do you see him?"

Rick heard the siren. "Let me check." He set the phone down and ran outside, saw a police car flying down the road toward him. He went back in. "Yes, he's here."

"More cars are on the way."

"Thank you," Rick said and hung up. He ran outside to meet the policeman. The patrol car pulled right behind his car at an odd angle. A small crowd started to form at the intersection.

The policeman got out of his car. "You the one called in the robbery?"

"Yes, I'm Rick Denton. This is my mom and stepfather's bookstore. He's in the hospital. I'm just here helping out."

"I'm Sergeant West. Let's go inside and have a look."

As they walked, the officer took out a notepad and began writing. Rick explained everything again to him. He heard more sirens outside. Through the doorway he saw two more police cars pull up. When he got to the part about suspecting that the thief was Columbo, he actually called him that.

"Columbo?" the officer said, smiling.

"No, I'm sorry. That's the nickname I gave him. There's a young lady works here part-time, Andrea. I think she called him JB or JD or something."

"So he's a local, not one of the transient homeless guys in town? We got quite a few down here from up north."

"I don't know. I guess so. I think she said he's been coming around for a year."

Sergeant West shook his head. "You sure it's him . . . this Columbo? Most of the locals don't do things like this. They know it's bad for getting handouts. And they know we know where they go."

"I can't say for certain. It was the high school kid who saw him."

"You said his name was Jed?"

"Yeah. But he described Columbo to a tee. And I know this guy. He's pretty sore at me. I chased him out of here, and Art, the guy who owns this store with my mom, he's been feeding this guy like a stray cat."

"I know a guy named JD," the officer said. "If it's him, shouldn't be too hard to track him down."

"Hey, wait," said Rick. "He's got a place right around the corner here, behind the church. What am I saying . . . a place. It's a stupid box." Rick walked outside and up the stairs. Sergeant West followed behind him. Two other officers walked up, and Sergeant West began to fill them in. As they talked, Rick went around the corner and found JD's box.

He bent down and looked inside. Stunk like booze and body odor. But it was empty.

Of course, it would be empty, Rick thought. He doesn't need to live here anymore. He's got plenty of money now.

24

Rick was angry now, outraged that this homeless parasite would break into a little bookstore that was barely making it, steal all their cash, possibly ruining his mother's livelihood. The creep was probably laughing his head off. Probably hadn't done a lick of honest work in years.

And what was Art thinking, feeding the bum like this? Letting this totally unstable guy hang around the store, maybe even putting his mother's life in danger. And Rick was angry as he thought about the hours of work it had taken putting that deposit together. How about all the hours he worked at the store generating sales, donating his time, the lost vacation days.

It was all gone. All because Columbo didn't get his stupid Egg McMuffin.

Besides the anger, Rick was definitely feeling some guilt. He should have brought the deposit bag with him to the diner. It was a stupid mistake, and he knew better. If he had, they'd only be out a few hundred dollars, not a few thousand. When Rick came back around the corner of the church to the sidewalk, two police cars sped off toward the south, the direction the high school kid said the homeless man went. He noticed the crowd had grown bigger. Now there were people across the street watching.

From out of the crowd, he heard Andrea's voice yelling, "Rick! Rick!" He saw her break through the crowd and run across the street. She yelled to Sergeant West. "Is Rick all right, the guy in the store?"

"I'm over here, Andrea."

She ran over. Seemed like she was about to give him a hug, but she stopped right in front of him. "What happened? Are you okay?"

"I'm fine. We got broken into while I was at the diner."

"Oh no. Did they take anything?"

"All the cash, including that big deposit."

"No," she said, her voice full of sympathy. "All of it?"

"Looks that way." They both walked toward the front door.

"Who are you, ma'am?" Sergeant West asked.

She introduced herself, and Rick explained her connection to the store.

"Haven't I seen you over at the diner round the corner?" he asked.

"I work here after I'm done there. I saw those two patrol cars leave."

"They're following a hunch," West said. "The guy took off on foot. Couldn't have gotten far. I wonder if one of you could go inside the store with me, just to double-check nothing else is missing."

"Sure," Andrea said. Sergeant West walked down the steps and into the store. Rick walked toward his car. "Where are you going?" she asked.

"Following my own hunch."

"Rick, don't go after this guy. We don't know if he's dangerous."

"I think I know who did it. That high school kid described him to me. Sounded just like Columbo . . . I mean JD."

Andrea shook her head. "It's not JD, Rick. It can't be him. He'd never do that. He loves Art."

"Maybe so, but he doesn't love me. And homeless people are capable of anything, Andrea. I'm just going to drive around downtown, see if I see him."

"If you do, please just call the police."

"I'll be back soon," he said, hopped in his car, and drove off.

◆

Rick had been driving slowly for twenty minutes throughout the downtown area, stopping anytime he saw a homeless person or a group standing around. He talked to quite a few; most ignored him, some answered questions he wasn't asking, disconnected from reality. The few he could understand said they hadn't seen JD all morning, wondered if Rick was some kind of cop. He was about to give up when he noticed a park near the water's edge on the north end of town. Must have been added since he left town years ago.

He pulled into a parking space under a live oak tree. From his car he scanned the view. Some kids played on the swing set. Moms sat nearby on a bench. A couple of college kids were walking around the fountain, holding hands. There was a small white building beyond the fountain that blocked his view of the area nearest the water. He got out and headed that way.

As he cleared the building, he saw a man in an overcoat about fifty yards away, walking along a white seawall that ran the river's edge. Flinging his arms around like he was arguing with the Invisible Man.

It's him.

Rick started running toward him. "JD!" he shouted.

JD stopped talking and looked around.

"JD," Rick yelled again, now too close for JD to miss where the sound was coming from.

When he saw Rick, he turned and started running in the other direction. But he wasn't fast, and Rick was on him in seconds. He leaped into the air and tackled him from behind. They tumbled on the grass. JD's face was pushed in the ground, but Rick could hear him screaming in panic. Rick rolled him over and was just about to unleash his rage in a flurry of punches to his face.

But he stopped short, his fist raised in the air.

The man's face was a mask of fear. He was babbling incoherently. "Please don't. Please help me. I won't do it anymore. I won't. I won't. But I can't stop. But I will, I promise. Please don't hit me. I'm sorry. I'm sorry. I'm sorry."

"Shut up!" Rick yelled into his face. He was sitting on top of him. JD stopped talking. "Where is it? Where's the money?"

"I don't, I don't have money. In my coat, my coat. There's some in my coat. Take it. Take it."

Rick got off him but kept him pinned down with one hand on his chest. He started going through his pockets, looking for the deposit bag and a wad of cash. All he found were four one-dollar bills crumpled up. "This isn't it," he yelled. "Where's the rest?"

"That's all I could get today. It's all. I can get some more later. I was too late for my McMuffin. You take it. I'll get more."

Wait a minute, Rick thought. Maybe he'd jumped the gun here. He looked back at his car, thought about how far the store was from here. He wasn't even sure JD could have walked this far since the break-in. He lifted his hand off his chest and reached back toward JD's feet and lifted his pant legs.

"What? What are you doing? Taylor? Where's Taylor? What are you doing?"

"Would you just shut up?" He hated touching the man's

filthy legs, but he didn't see a bruise on either shin. He squeezed his legs up and down, looking for a reaction.

He got one. JD started laughing, almost hysterically, crying, "Stop it, stop it!"

Rick stood up and reached out his hand. "Here, get up."

JD stopped laughing and looked up from the ground. "What now? What, what . . ."

"I'm not going to hurt you. It's obviously not you."

"It's not me? What's not me? Have you seen my friend Taylor?" he asked as Rick pulled him to his feet.

"No." Rick started walking away.

He got about ten steps when he heard JD yell out, "Since it's not me . . . can I come back tomorrow for my Egg McMuffin?"

"No!" Rick yelled without turning around.

25

Rick arrived back at the Book Nook to find Andrea sweeping up the broken glass. He noticed a fine black powder around the door, cash register, and counter. They had dusted for fingerprints. But the police were gone now. "Be careful," he said, looking down at the glass. Seemed like the thing to say.

She looked up. "Can you grab that dustpan over there and hold it here?"

"You were right, it wasn't him."

"What?"

"JD."

"You found him?"

Rick bent down and held the dustpan on the ground. "Yeah, but where I found him, he was too far away. He could never have gotten that far on foot in that short a time."

"I knew JD couldn't have done it. In his own way he cares about Art." She swept the glass into the dustpan.

"He also didn't have any bruises on his leg."

"What's that mean?"

"The kid with the skateboard saw the guy trip hard on the cement stairs out there. Ran off limping. JD didn't have any bruises."

Andrea stopped and looked down at him. "I probably don't want to ask how you found that out."

Rick smiled. "No, you probably don't." He walked the glass debris to the trash can outside and came back in. "How long we have to leave that black powder on there?"

"Sergeant West said I can clean it off whenever. Can I make a suggestion? Could you go to the hardware store down the street and get a windowpane while I clean up?"

"I can do that. You find anything else missing?"

"No. I think he just came for the cash." She walked the broom back.

The cash, Rick thought. What were they going to do? What was the right thing *to* do? It was his stupid mistake that allowed the thief to nab the deposit bag. Should he volunteer to reimburse that much to his mom? He'd have to check, but he knew it was twenty-two-hundred-something and change. A lot of dough. But a lot easier for him to come up with than his mom.

It made him so mad.

"What's the matter?" Andrea asked. She came back holding a soap bucket and rag.

"It's just so . . . frustrating. This guy gets to just walk in here and walk out with all that money." He had a thought. "Wonder if they have any insurance?" Maybe he'd just have to eat a small deductible.

"I don't know," she said. "Your mom might."

Rick sighed.

Andrea read the sigh. "We're going to have to call her about this."

"I'm dreading that. It's the last thing she needs, something else to worry about."

"Maybe you can search Art's office, see if you find a policy. Then you wouldn't have to call her just yet. See how much the insurance will cover."

"I'll do that, right after I get that windowpane."

Rick drove back with the windowpane carefully wrapped in newspaper sitting on the front seat. A little bag of things, putty, some tools. He hoped he could remember what the heck the hardware guy had said about how to fix it.

He hated hardware guys. Knew how to do everything that needs to be done. And the guy talked like everyone else should too. *"First, you take this thing here and then you do this with that thing there. But don't forget to make a notch in that thing first or this thing won't go in right. And you don't want that."* But he didn't say "thing," he used hardware words that, for some reason, Rick was supposed to already know.

His big fear was doing this whole repair project in front of Andrea, having to pretend that he knew what he was doing. He could just see himself forgetting one step or slipping in some way. The glass breaks. She looks over at him. And she'd know. *You have no idea what you're doing, do you? You're one of* those *guys.*

As Rick turned the corner and St. Luke's came into view, he saw two police cars parked beside the store. He sped up, wondering, What now? But their emergency lights were off. As he pulled into an open parallel parking spot, he saw the silhouette of a long-haired man's head and shoulders in the backseat of one of the squad cars. "All right," he said aloud. Looked like they got him.

He hopped out of his Celica and ran down the steps. "Is that him?"

Andrea was behind the counter, counting a stack of bills. Sergeant West stood on the other side. "About 99 percent sure," West said. "We get him booked, I'm sure his finger-prints will match the prints we took in here. Be nice if we got a positive ID from that high school kid. But I don't think we'll need him. I mean, look." He pointed to the counter.

"Even got the bank bag, with the deposit slip you made out for the store."

Rick hadn't seen it yet. "The money still in there?"

"I have to count it next," Andrea said. "But I peeked inside. Looks untouched."

"Happen to know how much was in the drawer?" West asked.

"I hadn't totaled it up yet," Rick said.

"It's 256 dollars," Andrea said. She finished counting the cash recovered from the drawer.

"There was probably a few dollars more," West said. "When we found him, he had an open bottle of vodka and a bag of burgers and fries from McDonald's. Might have been all the cash he spent."

"Where'd you find him?" Rick asked.

"Played a hunch," West said. "Sent one of my guys out to US-1. Told him to drive south toward the edge of town. Found him hitchhiking. These guys aren't too bright. My officer said, the way this guy looked, no one would have picked him up. Should have spent some more cash trading his filthy coat and clothes at a thrift store. Anyway, I knew it didn't sound like one of the local homeless guys. Figured after getting that much cash, he wouldn't hang around town."

"Very clever," Rick said. "You have no idea what a relief this is. It would have been a huge hit for this little store to lose that money." Rick looked at Andrea counting the money in the deposit bag. He couldn't remember the last time he'd felt so happy. "Is there anything I can do for you and your men?"

West looked around. "Don't see any donuts, so I guess not." He laughed, started making his way to the door.

"Wait." Rick pulled out his wallet. "Here." He handed the officer a twenty. "Please take it. I've gotta do something. Buy a couple rounds of drinks, you and your guys, when you're off duty."

"I'm sorely tempted, but really, I can't take your money." The officer shook Rick's hand and then left.

"It's all here," Andrea announced, holding up the bank bag. "Every last penny. Thank you, Jesus."

Rick wanted to run over and hug her. Almost felt like saying "Thank you, Jesus" too.

Almost.

26

The sun was setting, Leanne could tell. Sitting in a mostly dark room all day, she found it interesting how well the eye adjusts to the slightest nuances of light. She held her watch under the little book light. Good, Dr. Halper should be in soon. She'd reached a stopping place in her book and felt the need to stretch. She set the book down and walked over to Art.

She'd finally gotten to a calmer place about not being able to talk with him. She reached over and gently took his hand, remembering how much she loved it when he'd squeeze back. She loved that about Art—he was never afraid to show his affection. If they walked anywhere, they'd hold hands. If they sat next to each other, his arm would instantly go around her shoulder. He still said he loved her at least once a day, sometimes two or three.

He did, anyway . . . before last Friday. She stroked his hair with her finger. She knew he'd say it now if he could.

A tear slid down her cheek.

God, please let him stay.

"Excuse me, Leanne." It was Holly. "Your son Rick's on the phone, in the waiting room."

She wiped her cheek. "Seems like I always get calls when Dr. Halper's supposed to show up."

"I'll come get you if he does."

Leanne kissed Art on the forehead and headed for the waiting room. A woman about her age sat in a chair near the phone. She got up as Leanne entered the room. "I'll go, give you a little privacy," she said.

"You don't have to do that," said Leanne.

"I'm starting to get a little hungry anyway." She smiled and walked out the door.

Leanne picked up the phone. "Hi, Rick. How did your day go?"

"Safe to say like none I have ever had before."

"Really?" He sounded upbeat.

"Let's start with the headline. We were broken into just after lunch by this homeless guy. Took everything in the cash register and the bank deposit."

Leanne slid down in her chair. A panicked feeling wanted to form, but Rick didn't sound panicked. "Are you okay?"

"I wasn't there. I forgot my lunch again and locked the store up just long enough to go grab something. But that's not the best part."

"Best part?"

"We got it all back, Mom. Well, almost all. Guy bought some booze and McDonald's. But we counted the deposit money, and it's all here. In fact, I just dropped it off at the bank."

"Praise God," she said and breathed an audible sigh.

"Yeah, it's the craziest thing. And wanna hear something almost as crazy?"

"What?"

"I fixed the broken glass myself, didn't even screw it up."

She could tell he was really pleased with himself. She felt like she was listening to her little boy again, holding up a page, saying he'd colored between the lines. "That's great, Rick. So I guess they caught the fella who did it."

"They did. I thought for a while it was that guy JD. The one who hangs around here. But turned out it was some other homeless loser passing through town. They found him on US-1 trying to catch a ride south."

"I'm so glad."

"I've got to be honest with you though, makes me nervous, especially now, having this guy hanging around the store all the time."

"You mean JD?"

"Yeah. Art's got him fixated on these stupid Egg McMuffins. It's like he lives for them."

Leanne smiled. Art would have loved to hear that.

"You know," Rick said, "he's got his big ol' box right around the corner. That can't be good for business. Kind of says to any of these other homeless bums, 'Hey, over here.'"

"I'm not so sure it's hurting our business," Leanne said. "We're the only Christian bookstore in town. Seems like our customers are used to them. Most of them are harmless."

"Except the ones who rob you blind."

"You've got a point. But today's the first time we've been robbed since we started the store down there."

"Let's just hope we haven't started a trend," Rick said. "Why does the church let this guy live behind their building? Doesn't make sense to me."

"There's a few who don't like it, but they had a meeting a while ago. Art spoke up pretty strongly in JD's favor. He felt—"

"Why?"

"Well, it's an old church, in the old part of town, and that's where the homeless come. Art feels like some of them can still be reached."

"I don't see that happening," Rick said.

"You may be right," Leanne said. "But Art felt he was making some real progress with JD, thought he was worth the effort. I think so too."

"Well, he can pick right back up where he left off when he's better."

Leanne felt she better not push it. She was still hoping to make progress reaching Rick. "I'm praying that day comes soon."

"Any word?"

"I'm expecting to hear from the doctor any minute. Hold on . . ." Holly had just poked her head in the door, motioning that Dr. Halper was here. "I've got to go. The doc just arrived."

"Okay, well. You take care. Anything I can get you?"

"No. But really, what you're doing at the store, you have no idea how much that means to me." She said she loved him, thanked him again, and hung up the phone.

She walked around the nurses' station toward Art's room and found Dr. Halper at the foot of his bed, reading his chart. He was biting his lip and shaking his head. Leanne looked at Art. He seemed just the same.

"Oh, hi, Leanne," the doctor said quietly as she walked in. "I've got some good news. We're moving Art to Shands tomorrow."

"Tomorrow? I thought you said he needed another day or two."

"Well, I'd like another day or two, but it turns out we don't have that much time."

That didn't sound good. "What do you mean?"

"Dr. Valencia called me today. He's the neurosurgeon at Shands. He's been called on a consult in Atlanta and has to leave on Friday. That means we'd have to drive Art there tomorrow, try to get him stabilized again so he'd be ready for surgery first thing Thursday morning. Otherwise, we lose Dr. Valencia till Monday or Tuesday. I don't think Art can wait that long."

"You don't?"

"You know what I've already told you, Leanne." He put his hand gently on her shoulder. "There are no guarantees in something like this. We're working with odds and best-case scenarios. I'm just trying to give Art the best chance I can for his recovery. Getting him into the ambulance is a risk. The drive over is a risk. Getting him situated in a new hospital . . . you get the idea."

"It's all in God's hands, then," she said.

He nodded; he seemed sincere to her. Then he took another look at Art's numbers and wrote a few more notes on his chart.

27

Rick hung up the phone.

His mom had just told him about Art being sent to Shands this morning. They'd be putting him in the ambulance any minute. He felt bad for her; she sounded so afraid. She always tried to sound brave when she worried, even upbeat. *"It's all in God's hands. We have to trust him. I'm sure everything will be fine."* But he could tell by the tone of her voice, pauses in the wrong place, the sighs after each sentence.

He wasn't sure if this extra effort was for his sake or hers. Whatever the case, he still felt bad. He and Art weren't close, but Rick could tell . . . Art was her whole life.

A bell rang, just like it was supposed to. Worked like a charm. His second hardware achievement this week. He'd come in a half hour early this morning just to install it above the door. A little brass bell. Rick smiled and looked up at the front door.

But the man who'd walked in just now startled him. Big tall guy, probably six-four, all dressed in black. Rick zeroed in on a white spot under his chin. Oh no. It was a collar. This guy was a priest. He felt himself tense up.

"Well, hello, young man," the priest said as he cleared the two inside steps. He looked around the store. "Art here?"

"No," Rick said. "He's not."

The priest stepped inside. He had thick red hair parted on the side and wore a big smile. But still . . . he was a priest.

"Leanne?"

"No, she's not here, either. Just me."

The priest walked up to the counter. "And who might you be?"

"I'm Rick, Leanne's son. I live in Charlotte. I'm just down for a while to help out . . . *Father*."

The priest's face turned serious. "Actually, it's the Right Reverend. Or you may call me His Eminence. I'm not just a father, I'm a bishop."

"Oh . . . I'm sorry. I didn't know."

The priest's face broke into a wide grin. "Just messing with you, Rick." They shook hands. "I am a bishop, and some people in the church do call me things like that. But I hate it when they do. Your dad helped me get free of that stuff. You can call me what he calls me . . . Charlie."

"Actually, Art's not my dad." He didn't see how he could ever call this man Charlie. Except for the smile, he really did look like a Right Reverend.

"Your stepfather, then?"

"Yes, sir."

Father Charlie stood up straight. "Know when he'll be back?"

"Guess you haven't heard. Art's in the hospital. He's on his way to Shands right now, in Gainesville."

"Oh no," Father Charlie said.

Rick filled him in over the next few minutes, carefully choosing his words. The priest's face shifted through ever-increasing measures of concern. When Rick finished, he simply said, "My, my."

"The surgery is supposed to be tomorrow morning," Rick said.

"I need to check my schedule, see how soon I can get over there."

If Rick could get past the way the man looked, he seemed almost like a normal person. "Were you and my stepfather close?" It felt strange to Rick, calling Art that.

The priest leaned over the counter. "Not as close as I'd like to be, but I consider him a good friend. My job makes it hard sometimes. I have to see so many people it can be challenging to carve out enough time for deep friendships. But when we do get time together, I can always be myself. You have no idea what a gift that is."

He walked over to a short rack of greeting cards and slowly spun it around. "When I first came in here—must have been three years ago, around Christmastime then too—I was pretty uptight. See, even that . . . I would have never said *uptight* back then. That's Art. I had just been made a bishop, which made my life even more complicated. People already treated me like some untouchable holy man. Once they made me a bishop, even some of my fellow clergymen treated me the same. But not Art."

Rick started feeling uncomfortable with the direction this conversation was heading.

"Art didn't seem the least unsettled by me. I liked him right away. He invited me over to the couch back there, fixed me a cup of coffee. Fixed himself one and sat right next to me. Just started asking me questions. He didn't want anything from me, didn't want me to answer any deep theological questions. He just wanted to get to know me. See how I was doing. Pretty soon, I was telling him about the struggles I'd been having, things I'd only felt free to say to Alice. That's my wife."

Rick nodded. Then thought, You have a wife? His confusion must have been obvious.

"I'm not Catholic, if you're wondering," Father Charlie

said. "Only Catholic priests aren't allowed to get married. Anyway, I was telling Art how lonely and isolated I felt, always having to act this certain way around people, trying to figure out everyone's expectations, trying to live up to them. All the while, knowing deep inside, I couldn't do it. Nothing I tried ever seemed enough. And some people seemed to make it their aim to keep reminding me of that. Know what Art said?"

"No," Rick said with one eye on the bishop and the other on that little brass bell, hoping it would ring at any moment.

"Art said, 'What do people call you?' So I told him all the high-sounding religious titles I get in an average week. Then Art says, 'What would you like me to call you when you're in here?' And I said that, before all this, I used to be just Charlie. It's what my wife calls me when we're alone. From then on, Art started calling me Charlie. And he said, 'You know, Charlie, that's what Jesus calls you. You don't have to be anyone else with him than who you really are.' It was a wonderful thing."

Rick saw Father Charlie's eyes start to well up with tears. Father Charlie pulled a white handkerchief out of his coat pocket and wiped them away.

"After that, I started coming in here every chance I'd get. A few months later in the spring, we were talking and Art said, 'Charlie, you like fishing?' I hadn't been fishing since before college. So he said, let's go out together, he knew some great spots. And so we did. There's just something special about being out there in the morning. So quiet. The trees, the stillness of the water, all the different birds, the fresh air. It's just hard not to be at peace. But I remember this one time . . ."

Rick tried to stop himself from thrumming his fingers on the counter. He felt like he should be in a confessional. Why did people feel like they could bare their souls to him in here? It was a bookstore, for crying out loud.

"I was at a real low point, almost ready to leave the ministry.

I'd just had it up to here with people," he said. "People and all their problems. Always coming to me, as if I should instantly know what they need to make everything right. I mean, life is hard for ministers too. I need God just like they do. But by then I'd seen something different in Art . . . and Leanne too. People come in here all the time, from all different denominations and branches of the faith. I'd seen them open up to Art and Leanne, telling them all their problems."

You mean like you're doing right now, Rick thought.

"But people unloading their problems never seemed to bother them the way it did me. So out there fishing one morning, I asked Art about it, told him how I felt. You know what he said? He said, 'Charlie, how would you treat people if you knew you didn't have to fix them? If you knew that was God's job, and all he was asking of you was show them his love, maybe tell them some things he wanted them to know?'"

As Father Charlie said this, he looked up at the ceiling. Then he turned and looked right at Rick. "That conversation changed my life, Rick. We've been out fishing a number of times since then." He looked away, choking up again. "Lord, I hope he's all right. Poor Leanne must be worried sick."

"I think she is," Rick said. "I was just talking to her before you walked in. She's trying to be strong, but I can tell, she's really worried."

Father Charlie took a deep breath, composed himself. He picked out a card from the rack. "This one will do. But I'm not going to mail it, I'm going to take it over there myself. I'm going back to my office right now to free up some time. You wouldn't happen to know a number where I can reach your mom, would you?"

"I've got a number right here, Father. She just gave it to me." Rick wrote it on a slip of paper and handed it to him.

"Thanks, Rick, and please, you're family. Just call me Charlie." His big smile returned.

"Okay . . . Charlie." It didn't feel right at all.

Father Charlie set the card down by the register. It seemed to Rick like he was about to unload more of his heart. But then the little bell rang. A young mother was wrestling a stroller through the doorway. Her presence insured his visit with Father Charlie was at an end.

Saved by the bell.

28

Rick paid particular attention to his new little bell, especially after 2:30. Each time it rang, his heart rose and fell when Andrea didn't come through the door. It was now almost 3:30. She was much later than usual.

Good grief, what difference did it make when she got here? But if he didn't care, why did he keep staring at the door?

She's not right for you.

What are you thinking, are you nuts?

She's not like anyone you've ever gone out with.

She's beautiful, but thousands of women are beautiful.

She's not the casual dating kind; she'd want a serious relationship.

She goes to church because she likes to—and she has a kid.

Did you catch that . . . she has a kid.

You know what that means.

He did know.

If he got involved with Andrea, there was only one place the relationship could go. She was the marrying kind. She wouldn't get into a relationship with a man for anything less. He was certain of it. And that meant he'd have to become a stepfather someday to little Amy. Like Art was to him. He'd be the strange man coming in between a mother and her child. The unwanted intruder. The man she'd reject one day and grow up despising.

But he felt a strange reaction inside to these thoughts. Did he despise Art? Really despise him? Maybe a long time ago, but did he still? Art was a lousy businessman; Rick found that irritating. He thought back to the days when he *did* despise Art. What had Art really done to deserve his contempt?

He thought about this a good long while.

All he could come up with were a number of memories of Art trying to reach out to him, trying to create some kind of father-son bond. If Art was guilty of anything, it was of being too nice and trying too hard to win Rick over, and that he'd kept trying long after Rick had completely rejected him. Art had been guilty of not being Rick's real father. For Rick, it had been a capital offense.

He remembered a handful of times in high school when he'd gotten into trouble. There was Art, reaching out to him again. He'd start up these conversations about God, talking about the youth group down at their church and how much fun they had. About the third time this happened, Rick had said, "Quit trying to cram your religion down my throat!" He didn't know where he'd heard that. Probably on television. Seemed like an effective thing to say. And it worked. Art had stopped doing that too.

The bell rang. He looked up and smiled. It was Andrea, and right behind her Amy . . . *the kid*.

"Sorry I'm late," Andrea said.

"Hi, Mr. Rick," Amy said. She ran past her mom and past him down the aisle, carrying her doll in one hand, her handmade Christmas catalog in the other.

Rick looked at his watch then at Andrea. "Boy, you *are* late." He tried to act surprised.

She walked over to the counter, set her purse down behind it. "Amy's sitter called just as I was leaving the diner, said her daughter was home sick and she didn't want Amy to catch it. I had to pick Amy up at school, then tried getting her another sitter for almost an hour. I'm sorry I had to bring her. I had no other choice." She looked upset.

Rick walked over, stood on the other side. "It's okay, Andrea. Really. You can bring her here every day after school if you want. I don't mind." Had he really said that? Then he went further. "I like Amy." He really did like her. But that's not why he said it. He was trying to make an impression on Andrea. He had to stop this.

"Thanks, Rick. That's very kind." She took a deep breath, like she was trying to calm down. "Your mom and Art offered the same thing, quite a few times. But Amy really likes going to her friend's house after school. And I like her to go. She gets to do little girl things over there. Here she mostly just has to behave."

"You still seem a little upset. Anything wrong?"

She looked away then reached for a tissue under the counter. "I'm worried sick about Art. Have you heard anything?"

"No. But they should be at Shands by now. I'm sure if anything went wrong, she'd have called. I've been going on no-news-is-good-news all day."

Andrea dabbed her eyes. "I'm sure you're right. Hope you are. One of my regular customers could tell I was off today. A few minutes later, he's telling me his uncle had an aneurysm and died from a second bleed a week later."

"What an idiot."

"Well, I guess it's just what happened."

"Maybe so, but that's not something you say to somebody who's worried sick."

"No, it's not." She looked like she could use a hug. "Isn't the surgery tomorrow morning?"

"That's what Mom said. But Andrea, Art's in the best of hands. She said the whole reason his doctor wanted him there was because this guy's the best surgeon in the southeast."

"I know."

The Christmas music stopped. "I'll get that." He walked toward the back. He put the cassette marked #2 in the player. It began with "Silent Night." Might help calm her down.

"Mr. Rick, look, I'm almost done."

He walked over and sat on the couch next to Amy. "Let me see. Wow, look how thick it is." He wanted to say something about her doll but couldn't remember its name.

"Annabelle's been very patient," Amy said. "I told her she couldn't look at it until it was ready. I only have a few more pictures to paste." She leaned over and whispered so her doll couldn't hear. "I couldn't finish it 'cause I left the Penney's catalog here last time. Then my mom kept forgetting to bring it home."

"Is your mom always forgetting things?"

"No, not always. But she's been real worried lately."

"You're a good little girl." Such a cliché thing to say. "She must be worried about Art's surgery."

"That and one more thing, I think."

"Really, what else?"

She leaned over and whispered again. "She didn't really tell me, but I heard her praying last night in her bedroom. I came in to ask for a drink. She was telling God she needed more money but didn't know where to get it."

"More money?"

"She said she's afraid she'll have to get a third job at night, but she didn't want to leave me any more than she already does." She sat back and pulled Annabelle close. "I don't want her to leave me any more, either."

Rick looked down at her catalog lying open on the coffee table. The left page was blank, awaiting, he supposed, the final two cutouts from the Penney's catalog. But on the right page Amy had pasted an ad for Disney World, and above it, she'd written "Mommy." "What's this one?" he asked.

Amy leaned toward him again and whispered. "That's what Annabelle wants to get Mommy for Christmas."

"Your mom wants to go to Disney World?"

Amy nodded.

"How does Annabelle know?"

"We asked her. Last week. I said, 'What do you want for Christmas?' And she said she didn't want anything. I said, everybody wants something for Christmas. I asked her to just pretend. If she could have anything she wanted, what would it be?" She pointed to the Disney World ad and whispered, "She wants to go to Disney World and go on nothing but E-ticket rides the whole time."

Just then Andrea came walking toward them. Amy closed her catalog. "Okay, you two," Andrea said, "no fair telling secrets."

"I was just asking Amy what you wanted for Christmas," Rick said.

"Rick, you better not get me anything for Christmas."

"Why not?"

"I don't even know where I'm getting Christmas money for—" She paused. "Let's just don't, okay?"

"Fair enough. But how about you let me take you and Amy out for dinner after we close up here? You've had a rough day. I'm sure you don't want to go home and have to cook after this."

"Can we, Mom?"

"I don't think so."

"Please, Mom."

"C'mon, Andrea. It would be great for me too. Not having to eat alone again."

She thought about it a moment. The little brass bell rang. "I better go up front." She turned and walked away.

Rick quickly followed and stopped her halfway down the aisle. "Don't think of it as a date, Andrea," he said quietly. "Just a meal between friends."

"I . . . I don't think so, Rick. Maybe another time." She seemed to force a smile then walked toward the counter.

Rick stood there confused. Almost stunned.

He hadn't even considered the possibility of being turned down.

▲

"Put your seat belt on," Andrea said, instantly regretting her edgy tone. She turned on the car.

"Why didn't you say yes to Mr. Rick?" Amy asked. "We haven't been out to eat . . . forever."

"I know that," she snapped. She pulled the car onto the street. She didn't look over but could almost feel Amy wilting beside her. "I'm sorry."

Amy sat up and turned around. "Then it's not too late. There he is now, just locking up the store. We can still turn around."

"No, Amy, we can't. I didn't apologize for saying no to Mr. Rick. I apologized for the way I talked to you."

Amy plopped back down in her seat. "So why did you?"

"Why did I what?"

"Why did you say no?"

One day Andrea hoped she and Amy could talk like friends, but they were nowhere close to that now. "It's just hard to explain. I didn't want to give him the wrong . . ."

"You didn't want him to think you like him?"

Is she already able to catch things like this? "In a way, yes."

"But don't you like Mr. Rick?"

"I do but—"

"So why not say yes?"

Andrea looked at her, the edginess subsiding. She tried to

read her eyes. She could tell that Amy really was too young to grasp the situation. She couldn't think of any collection of words that would help her understand.

Or, for that matter, any words that would help her with her own feelings right now.

29

A wasted moon.

Far too beautiful to be viewing alone.

It had begun to rise above the horizon two hours ago, all of its light perfectly contained within the borders of a glowing orange sphere. Except for a shimmering golden path that rolled out across the sea to the water's edge. It was mesmerizing. He could see the outline of every crater on the lunar surface.

Rick was sitting on a sand dune three blocks down the beach from the Howard Johnson's. His bare feet felt cool in the soft white sand. A night breeze rustled across the dunes, swishing through the sea oats like the wind through a field of wheat. The calming influence was aided by tiny waves that lapped against the shore.

A fried clam dinner from HoJo's sat heavy in his stomach—the third clam dinner he'd eaten this week. If Andrea had agreed to join him for dinner, he'd have taken them someplace nice. Maybe the new steakhouse out by the highway or Abe's Crab Shack right on the water down by the inlet.

But she said no.

He had failed. Frozen clams, shipped in from HoJo Central

HQ, thawed and fried in a vat of day-old grease, was his punishment.

But he knew why Andrea had said no. The reason was as obvious as the full moon staring back at him. She was a grown-up. He was not. She wasn't looking for short-term adventures, moments of happiness with no strings attached. That had been a basic requirement for all the girls he'd dated. And there had always been a strong and steady supply. Especially since he'd started making serious dough.

Andrea was almost broke, by the sounds of it. Thinking of taking a third part-time job just to buy her daughter a few Christmas presents. She wasn't stupid; she knew Rick was loaded. She had a lot to gain by saying yes.

But still she said no.

He stood up. The moon was high overhead now. He brushed the sand off his pants and walked down the dune. He should just let it go. He wasn't planning on sticking around. As soon as Art got past this surgery thing and was well enough for his mom to come back to the store, Rick would be out of here, back to Charlotte where he belonged. Why did he even care?

But he did care.

As he walked along the edge of the dunes, felt the breeze blowing at his back, he realized he cared a lot. He was keenly aware of a strong desire beginning to form inside him. He wanted to become the kind of man someone like Andrea would say yes to.

30

Yesterday had been terrifying for Leanne.

It was the day they had moved Art from the little hospital in Seabreeze to Shands, the huge teaching hospital in Gainesville, almost three hours away. Every time the ambulance turned a corner, at every traffic light, at the slightest noise or smallest bump, she'd tense up and stare at Art. Afraid if his eyes opened, the shock of the situation might instantly cause another bleed in his brain and kill him.

An RN and a paramedic had ridden in the back of the ambulance with her, monitoring his vital signs the entire way. They had remained steady. She wondered how many alarm bells might have gone off if they'd hooked her up to the same machines.

Shortly after they'd arrived at Shands and admitted Art to their ICU, Dr. Valencia had surprised her with a visit. She instantly liked him. He was tall, maybe ten years younger than her, with thick dark hair that turned gray along the edges. He seemed to sense her anxiety, asked how the ride over had been. When she'd told him of her fears, he told her he was sorry no one had informed her, but that Art had been heavily sedated before making the trip. They didn't want him to awaken, either.

Leanne had asked if Art would remain sedated until his surgery, and the doctor said probably not. They just wanted to keep him that way until Dr. Valencia could confirm that Art had stabilized from the trip. He'd asked her if she wanted something to help her sleep.

It was now a little past seven in the morning. Sitting there next to Art, less than thirty minutes before they would bring him to the operating room, she was glad she'd accepted Dr. Valencia's offer. She never would have slept last night, with all the thoughts and fears colliding in her head. The greatest was also the most obvious . . . and the most dreaded. Would Art survive the surgery? Would her last conversation with him on earth be the chat about nothing last Friday morning as he'd headed out the door? Had her last kiss been that peck on the cheek?

"Can I get you something, Mrs. Bell? Some water, coffee?"

Leanne looked up at the pleasant face of the nurse who'd been looking in on Art for the last twenty minutes. About an hour ago, they had taken Art from the ICU and wheeled him into this holding room on a different floor, to prep him. "Do you have any orange juice?"

"I think I can manage that. Anything else?"

"I'm not hungry."

"If you change your mind, just let me know. Did they say how long your husband would be in surgery?"

"Dr. Valencia said he couldn't be sure until things got underway, but it would be at least three or four hours."

"Dr. Valencia's the best. I've seen him work miracles."

"Thanks." Leanne managed a smile. The nurse turned and walked away. Leanne sighed then looked back at Art.

His eyelids fluttered. She must have imagined it. She sat up, staring at them for several moments.

Nothing. She sat back.

A few moments later, he squeezed her hand. It startled

her, felt almost like an electric shock. She looked back at his eyes. Nothing.

They fluttered again. "Art," she whispered, leaning forward. "Art . . . can you hear me?"

His eyes blinked, then opened just a little.

Her face became hot; she felt a rush of emotions. It took all her strength not to yell out loud. Calm down, she told herself. She took a deep breath. "I'm here, Art. It's Leanne. I'm right here. Squeeze my hand if you can hear me."

He did.

Tears fell down her face. He understood. She should go tell someone, maybe get the nurse. He blinked a few more times then opened his eyes wider and turned his head, looking to one side then the other.

"You're okay, hon," she said. "You're in the hospital. But I'm right here. Squeeze my hand again if you understand me." Keep squeezing back, she thought. Don't ever stop.

"Leanne," he said feebly.

She reached out her other hand and gently stroked his cheek. "Right here, Art." She tried to remember the instructions Dr. Halper had told her at the beginning. *Try to keep him calm. Don't talk about anything that will make him think too deeply. He probably won't remember what happened.*

"Where are we?" His voice sounded a little stronger. His eyes seemed to be focusing on hers.

"We're at Shands Hospital in Gainesville."

"Gainesville?"

"You had a little accident. Well, not an accident. A sudden illness."

"A stroke?"

She shook her head no. "It was an aneurysm. You know what that is?"

He nodded.

"The doctor says it's very important that you remain

absolutely calm, so your brain doesn't bleed again." He seemed to understand. "It happened six days ago, the day after Thanksgiving. Do you remember?"

"No. Six days ago. Have I been lying here that long?" His voice was quiet but clear and steady.

"You've been in bed that long, but mostly in our little hospital back home. The doctor there wanted you to come here for the operation. He said the surgeon here is the best he's ever seen."

She saw his throat swallowing, felt him squeeze her hand harder. "When?" he asked.

"This morning, in a little while." She hated saying such things to him. She didn't want him to worry. She wished somehow she could just make it all stop. He was back now. She didn't want it to end.

"I'm sorry," he said.

"Don't be sorry, Art."

"For putting you through this. Must have been so hard for you."

"I just missed you so much. That's been the hardest part."

He smiled.

"Why are you smiling?"

"You look so beautiful."

She looked away. "I don't, my hair—"

"Looks great to me."

He always said that, even on her worst hair days. He looked past her, above her head. She turned to see what he was looking at. A little Christmas tree sat on a shelf on the wall behind her, maybe eighteen inches tall.

"Like the one on the counter at the store," he said.

She nodded, happy he remembered. "Well, you'll have to get better real quick, so we can celebrate Christmas together." She was about to tell him how Rick had come down to help at the store but stopped. It might stir his mind the wrong way. He never talked about it much, but she knew their lack of relationship had always made him sad.

"I'd like that." He squeezed her hand again then reached out for her with his other hand. The IV tube held him back. "Got me on a short leash," he said.

Still has his sense of humor, she thought.

"Listen, hon," Art said. "There's something I need to say."

She looked in his eyes. She knew what it was. *Don't say it.*

"I know how serious these things can be. I'm sure the doctor has told you."

She took a deep breath.

"Don't know what God has for us here, my love. Could be nothing or could be the last time we'll be able to talk for a long—"

She put her fingers gently over his lips. "Don't say it, Art. Please."

With his free hand, he gently pulled her hand away. She looked down. "I have to, Leanne. Just in case. Look at me."

She lifted her head.

"I hope I come back from this in one piece. But in case God has other plans, I just want you to know . . ." Tears welled up in his eyes. "You have made me so happy . . . for so many years. Marrying you has made me a rich man."

"Art, please stop."

"You're the finest woman I've ever known. You've been a gift from God to me."

Leanne couldn't help it. She burst into tears and rested her head on his chest. "I love you" was all she could say. He patted her head gently.

"Is everything okay?"

Leanne looked up. It was the nurse holding her orange juice.

"Mr. Bell, you're awake."

Art smiled at her, blinking back his own tears. "It would

seem so. Do you know for how much longer . . . till the surgery?"

The nurse looked at her watch. "You have a few more minutes. Here, I'll set this down and leave you two alone."

Leanne reached over and took a sip. It tasted so good. "Wish I could give you some," she said.

He held up his IV hand. "Just pour a little in here."

She smiled.

"Finish up your juice and lay your head back down here," he said, patting his chest. "I want to hold you as long as I can. For at least a few minutes more."

31

"I know he looks terrible, Mrs. Bell, but really, it went very well in there."

Leanne could barely look at Art; his head was completely wrapped in bandages, tubes sticking out everywhere. More machines than she'd ever seen. "He's okay?"

"For now," Dr. Valencia said. "He's still in critical condition. Dr. Halper said he briefed you on the situation."

"He did," Leanne said. Dr. Halper stood beside her.

"But here, at this point, things are good. His vitals stayed strong throughout the surgery. We had no surprises. We found the aneurysm right about where we expected. Everything went according to plan."

"Thanks again, Doctor, for letting me observe," Dr. Halper said.

"You're welcome."

"Do you know when he'll wake up?" she asked. "When the anesthesia will wear off?"

"He's not going to wake up for quite a while," Dr. Valencia said. "Maybe a day or two. But that's my doing. There's going to be a lot of swelling from the surgery, and we want his brain to be completely still until we're sure the initial danger is past."

"Is he in a coma?" she asked.

"An induced coma, but when we're sure he's stable, we'll slowly bring him back. Someone told me he woke up just before the surgery."

"He did," Leanne said. "Is that a good sign?"

"Can be," the doctor said. "My hope is that he'll wake up very soon after we take him off all sedation. But you know it's still going to be a challenging situation for several more weeks."

"Do you have any idea when I can bring him home, to our hospital in Seabreeze?"

"Can't say for sure right now, but I'm hoping in three or four days."

Three or four days. She wasn't thinking she'd have to be here that long.

"I have to leave now, Mrs. Bell. But I've asked Dr. Halper to brief you a little further, let you know what to expect in the days ahead."

"Thank you so much for taking Art's case," Leanne said, holding back tears.

Dr. Valencia gave her a gentle hug then left her with Dr. Halper. "Let's go back to the waiting room, where we can sit," Dr. Halper said as they walked down the hall. "That was an amazing sight to see, watching him work, I mean. I'm glad we did this."

That made her feel good. It was the most upbeat she'd seen him so far. The waiting room was large, three times the size of the one at Seabreeze. They sat in the chairs near the door, away from most of the people and the television.

"Dr. Valencia thought it would be wise to give you a little more information than I gave you back home. They've done a lot more of these surgeries here and know a little more about the different things that can happen from this point."

Leanne found herself tensing up, not responding so much to his words but his eyes and the tone of his voice.

"I'm not telling you these things because they *will* happen, only because they can. And he feels—we feel—it's better for you to know up front."

She didn't feel good anymore.

"In most surgeries when things have gone this well, we have all kinds of hope and can say things we doctors love to say to families. But when you're working with the brain, there's still so much we don't know and a lot more potential for surprises."

"Like what?" She just wanted him to say whatever he was building to.

"Like . . . the bleeding. How will it affect other areas of his brain? Some people who recover well from the surgery still have other complications. Some people experience personality changes, some short-term memory loss. Some people complain of not being able to do things they did all the time before. He may need therapy, if certain areas of the muscular or nervous system have been affected."

"Dr. Halper, things like this would be like music to my ears right now. I just don't want him to die."

He smiled. "I understand, Leanne. I can't say just yet that won't happen, but he's in the '20 percent club' right now."

"Is that good?"

"Eighty percent of the patients who've had what Art's had have already died by this point. So I'm starting to get hopeful. Which is why I'm trying to prep you for what the 20 percent who survive often face."

That sounded hopeful. "I'm willing to face anything if I get to do it with Art beside me."

He stood up. "I'm going to stick around today, check in on him throughout the day. Then maybe head back to Seabreeze tonight."

She got up and gave him a big hug. "Thank you so much, Dr. Halper. You've taken such great care of us."

After he left, she went back to look at Art. The poor thing. He looked so helpless lying there. "Lord," she prayed, "just bring him back to me. Thank you for bringing him through the worst of it. I'm willing to go through whatever you have in mind. Just please bring Art back."

▲

"He made it, Mom? That's great." Rick was actually relieved. He looked across the counter at Andrea. Her face lit up, reacting to the news. They had been just about to close when his mom called, reversing the charges.

"He looks terrible," Mom said.

"Is he awake?"

"No, but he woke up for the first time just before the surgery. I actually got to talk with him a few minutes."

Rick held his palm over the phone and told Andrea.

"He woke up, really?" Andrea said. "Is he awake now?"

Rick shook his head. "So what are they saying?" he asked his mom.

"That's part of the reason I'm calling, Rick. They're saying he's still in critical condition. He probably won't even wake up for a day or two. And then they're going to keep him here at least another day or two after that."

Rick knew why she'd said this, why it bothered her. "Don't worry about it, Mom."

"But your work . . . I won't be home till Monday, maybe Tuesday. Then they'll just be moving him to our hospital, and I don't know what to expect after that."

Rick had already thought this through. You don't have brain surgery then get out of bed in a day or two. "Let me worry about that, Mom. I've got vacation time saved up. Just take care of Art and yourself. You got a place to sleep while you're there?"

"I'm just going to stay in Art's room, I think."

161

"That's gotta be murder on your back, all this time."

"It's nothing like my bed at home, but I wouldn't sleep at all there. At least I manage a few hours when I'm near him."

Rick didn't know what to say. He'd never given it much thought before, but he had to admit, their love for each other was impressive. "Anything I can do?"

"You've already done more than you know. You've taken such a load off my mind. Thanks so much for coming, Rick."

Rick said good-bye and hung up the phone, filled Andrea in on what his mother had said, and tried not to think about the phone call he knew he'd have to make tomorrow . . . asking his boss for another week off.

Leanne couldn't put her finger on it, but Rick seemed different somehow. Good different. She turned the corner out of the ICU waiting room and walked down the long hall that led to Art's room. They'd moved him there about an hour ago.

As she looked up, a great commotion was taking place at the end of the hall. Doctors and nurses rushed toward the same room, and someone wheeled a cart right behind them.

Oh no. It looked like Art's room.

She began to jog down the hall.

It *was* Art's room.

32

Rick had spent the entire day at the store, actually worrying.

Totally unlike him.

The smaller part of his struggle was that he'd tried to call his boss that morning but learned he wouldn't be available until 3:00 p.m. Rick had wanted to get this thing over with. Instead, he spent the unguarded moments of the day rehearsing different ways to say his bit, each one altered by different reactions his boss might have.

But his greater struggle came from the news about Art. His mom had left an urgent message at the Howard Johnson's last night to call her at Shands as soon as he could. He'd gotten in around 7:00 p.m. after eating another dinner alone. It sounded like they'd almost lost him. Rick still didn't quite get what happened, but Art's vital signs had started crashing, and it took drastic measures to save him. He had stabilized somewhat since then, from what Mom had said in her call this morning.

She was still so upset; Rick thought he should close up the store and drive to Gainesville. But Father Charlie had called an hour later, saying he was on his way. Rick was sure Father Charlie would do more good for his mom than he could, so he changed his mind.

But that left him sitting in the store all day, with little else to do but think. He was actually happy every time the bell rang and a customer came in. Fortunately, none of the more eccentric ones had shown up. Rick felt he could manage the fake smiles and necessary Christmas cheer for the average customers, but didn't think he could muster the kind of energy required to handle the crazies.

He looked at his watch. It was time. He picked up the phone and dialed the firm's number, asked the receptionist to put him through to Mr. Rainey.

"Rick, how's it going down in sunny Florida?"

"It's . . . sunny all right, Mr. Rainey. How are things back home?"

"Getting pretty busy, but you know that. Happens every year. Everybody's moving slow coming back from Thanksgiving, and now all the year-end stuff is starting to kick in. Got to get it all done before the Christmas vacations start up. You wrapping things up at that store?"

Rick had hoped for at least a few minutes of small talk before jumping in. "Not exactly, sir. That's why I'm calling."

"Oh?"

"My stepfather's surgery was yesterday. He came through it okay, but there's been some complications."

"So, what's that mean?" His voice had an edge.

"I guess it means that if he survives these next few days, he's going to be stuck in the hospital a while, and my mom will be stuck there with him."

"And you're saying you'll be stuck in that store down there a while longer."

"Afraid so, sir."

"How long?"

"Probably another week."

"You said a week last week."

"I know. I still have two more weeks of vacation time left."

"You know that's not the point, Rick. I'm sure you didn't plan on taking it now, leaving all your clients hanging out to dry. We've got a ton of work to get through before the Christmas holiday."

"I know, Mr. Rainey. But what else can I do?"

"I guess you gotta do what you gotta do, Rick. But so do I."

"What's that mean, sir?"

"It means I'm going to have to let some other guys take care of your clients while you're gone. We can't lose anyone—we *won't* lose anyone—because you've got a personal situation down there. And Rick, you know the guys we hired. They're like you, top-notch guys who know their stuff, know how to win people over."

Rick knew what that meant. He might lose half his client list, or more, if he did this. "I understand, Mr. Rainey."

"Well, as long as you do . . . I guess that's all there is to say. Have a great week. Hope you get something to show for it." And he hung up.

Hope you get something to show for it. That was the thing, wasn't it? Rick had a sick feeling inside.

The feeling he had just committed career suicide.

33

Leanne had settled down somewhat from all the terror she'd felt immediately after things started going wrong. She still didn't understand everything she'd been told. All she knew was that Art had done well through the surgery yesterday and for several hours after. Something complicated happened yesterday evening, and he'd almost died.

She was sitting beside Art now in the ICU, watching all the activity in the hall through the glass dividing wall. Dr. Halper had just left. He had been so kind. He'd changed his plans and stayed overnight to keep an eye on Art. He'd explained that Art had finally stabilized, but to a lesser place than where he'd been right after surgery. His blood pressure was still dangerously low. If he didn't begin to respond to the meds they were giving him, he could be in serious trouble. He said he hated to leave her but had numerous patients back home to tend to.

Leanne was tired of sitting. She stood next to his bed, in the one place she could stand because of all the machines and tubes. Several of them were new or newer versions of ones back home, and she had no idea what they were doing. But she understood the blood pressure monitor just fine. She looked at it every few seconds.

Right now it read 63 over 41. She knew 120 over 80 was considered normal, so Art's numbers were half what they should be. She reached for his free hand and gave it a squeeze. She tried to remember what it felt like yesterday morning when he squeezed back. She had been fighting off thoughts all day that God had just allowed Art to wake up like that to say good-bye.

"Leanne?"

She turned at the familiar voice. "Charlie!" There he was, Father Charlie, filling the doorway. He walked toward her, holding out his arms. She fell into them and released all her pent-up fear and emotion.

"It's all right, Leanne. You just let it out." He patted her gently on the shoulders.

She continued to cry for several minutes. She didn't mean to, it just happened, seeing a good friend. "Oh my," she heard him say. She leaned back. He was looking over her shoulder at Art. They parted and he walked to Art's side.

"Oh Art. My good friend." Tears welled up in his eyes. "Alice would be here with me, but she's up north taking care of her mother." He looked up at all the monitors. He seemed bewildered by the sight. "So what's the latest? What are the doctors saying?"

Leanne filled him in as best she could. She got to the last part and pointed toward the blood pressure monitor. "That's the one they're watching the most," she said.

"That's Art's blood pressure?" he asked. It read 59 over 39.

"It's so low," she said. "They said if it doesn't get up to more normal levels, we'll lose him."

Charlie shook his head. "We can't have that. Not after all this. I can't believe God intends to take him after bringing him through the worst of it."

"I hope you're right," she said.

"Leanne, I don't know what's come over me, but I just feel

like I'm supposed to lay hands on him and pray, you know, like they do in the Bible."

She had never heard Charlie talk like this. She wasn't sure the church tradition he came from even believed in that sort of thing. She noticed a small black book in his hands. It wasn't a Bible.

He noticed her looking at it. "I'm going to set this thing over here," he said, laying the book on a small counter. "The prayer I'm going to pray isn't in that prayer book. Why don't you come over here with me? You hold his hand, and I'll lay my hands on him, nice and gentle."

She did. Then he pointed to the blood pressure monitor. "What should those numbers say?"

"What?"

"What numbers are the doctors saying they need to see on that monitor for Art to be out of danger?"

She looked up at the monitor. "He said that 40 has to get up to about 75 and that 62 has to get closer to 100. He said that's what they're hoping for."

"Well, Leanne, I know this may sound crazy. But I've been praying for Art the whole drive over. Just talking to God out loud. In between, I've been remembering all the good times we've had and all the wonderful things I've learned from him. The more I did this, the sadder I got. By the time I got here, I was feeling like I was coming here to say good-bye. When I first walked in and saw him like this, I was sure of it. But something's come over me, and I don't believe that anymore."

"What do you believe?"

"Watch that monitor." He closed his eyes. "Father in heaven, forgive me for being so bold, but I'm thinking I'm feeling this way because of you, something you're doing here. I just can't believe you mean to take my friend Art just now. Seems to me if it was his time, you could have taken him that first day, or any of the days in between. Or not let him make it through the surgery."

"Look." Leanne couldn't believe it. Art's numbers started climbing. The 62 now read 70, and the 40 now said 58.

"Then let's keep going," he said. "Father, Leanne needs Art back in her life. And so do all the folks down at the Book Nook. And all the folks over at their little church. And I need Art in my life, Alice and I both do. So please, dear Lord—"

"Look!" Leanne said. "They're going up more every time you talk!"

Charlie opened his eyes. Art's blood pressure read 91 over 69. "Then I'll keep talking. Thank you, Father, for doing this. Thank you for reminding me you can do all things. I must have told other people that a thousand times, but I'm seeing it right before my eyes."

97 over 72.

Leanne burst into tears of joy. God was doing it. It was a miracle.

"Lord, would you bring these numbers all the way back to where they need to be, and then keep them there so Art can start to get better. Thank you so much. In Jesus' name, amen."

101 over 76.

Leanne turned to Charlie. "You did it." She gave him a big hug.

"He did it," Charlie said, his index finger pointing upward.

"I know *he* did it," she said. "But he used you. It's like you saved Art's life. You stay here. I'm going to go get the doctor."

34

As he walked the beach early in the morning, Rick was beginning to find it easier to have positive thoughts about God. He'd actually talked to God several times, feeling almost sure he was being heard. The news from his mom about Art's sudden turnabout with Father Charlie had certainly helped. And of course, it was almost easy to think about God while watching a glorious sunrise come up over the water, seeing its brilliant rays fan out through the clouds across the sky. Seeing the vastness of the ocean, pondering the source of endless waves breaking on the beach.

But this was more than a live nature show. Something was going on inside him.

When he awoke that morning, he'd expected to feel dread inside as he considered his job situation. Mr. Rainey had been his hero, his mentor, the man he'd wanted to model his career after. Rainey had it all. He could afford any one of these beautiful beach houses or the mansions Rick saw every morning driving over the bridge. And Rainey didn't drive a Celica like Rick; he drove a ritzy, high-end Jaguar that cost as much as Rick's small condo.

Everything Rick had done, every decision he'd made in the last five years, was to get in good with Rainey and stay there.

Let Rainey lead him all the way to the promised land. Yet here Rick had been willing to let it all go in a single telephone conversation, and for what?

Hope you get something to show for it.

These words kept repeating in his mind as he walked along the water's edge. He stopped for a moment and watched a little sandpiper running along the wet sand, pecking at the seaweed. It waited till the last moment when the water came rushing toward it, then fled, its little feet moving as fast as a hummingbird's wings. It waited till the water subsided then rushed back to the seaweed once again.

It's what all sandpipers did. This was their life. Rick felt right then that it was a picture of his life back in Charlotte.

The bigger question for him now was . . . what would he have to show for it at the end? He ran from everything and anything in his life that truly mattered, and he'd been running like this as long as he could remember. With occasional moments to peck at some seaweed. That was the prize.

But this morning was different. Rick didn't wake up with the feelings of doom and dread he'd expected. Instead he felt . . . relief. Even freer somehow. He'd felt this sense of freedom the entire time he'd been walking along the beach.

These fine feelings continued to surround him as the morning went on, as he got ready to head to the store, as he ate his breakfast, as he traveled all the way across the bridge into the old, run-down downtown area. Right up until he pulled into his parking place next to the Book Nook. But then he saw that Columbo was back, peeking his head around the corner.

He's back for his stupid Egg McMuffin, he thought.

Rick got out of the car and was just about to yell at him when Andrea pulled in behind him.

"Wait, Rick," she shouted. She got out of the car, clutching a little white bag. "JD, don't go. I've got your sandwich right here, and some hash browns to go with it."

Rick couldn't believe it. What was she thinking? He closed his door, hard.

JD stepped out around the corner, a big smile on his face. He turned his head and said to no one, "See, Taylor, I told you she'd come."

It was ridiculous. JD didn't look at Rick, just Andrea. Rick turned from the scene, walked down the steps, and unlocked the door. Behind him he heard her say, "You sit tight, and I'll bring out your coffee in a few minutes."

He turned the lights on, set his lunch behind the counter, and started going through the morning setup routine.

"Morning, Rick," she said.

"Morning," he said back. He plugged in the Christmas lights, popped in the Christmas music cassette. He noticed she went right to the coffeepot. Good, let her fix it.

This was going to be a problem in their relationship. Then he caught himself. *You idiot, you have no relationship.* He walked back to the office and took care of a few bookkeeping things that needed his attention. He heard her out there, doing this and that, humming, occasionally singing along with a familiar carol. Smelled the fragrant aroma of coffee. Heard her fix the coffee. Listened for the little bell to ring and knew she was bringing JD his promised cup.

When he heard her come back, he figured it was safe to come out and talk this over. He walked around the counter and sat on the little stool. He looked at her, his anger quickly muted by the look on her face. It was pure kindness.

"Before you say anything, Rick, let me explain."

She was so beautiful.

"I was just so happy last night after we got your mom's call. After being worried sick all day that we were going to lose Art, the way God brought him back . . . I don't know. For the first time, I was sure he was going to make it."

Rick didn't see how this connected to Egg McMuffins. "I was happy too," he said.

"Well, after we locked up, I was driving through town toward my apartment when I saw poor JD walking by himself down by the park. I just remembered how much Art cared about JD, all the effort he made to reach out to him, and I just felt bad."

"Bad that I've pushed him out?"

She looked away from him. "Yes. I know you think it's the right thing to do."

"Andrea, it's just . . . the guy is homeless. He smells. He lives in a box. He talks to himself."

"I know. And Art knew that, but he didn't care. I don't care."

"That homeless guy broke into the store, stole everything. If that cop hadn't caught him before he left town, where would we be right now?"

"I know," she said. "But that wasn't JD. Not all homeless people are the same. Just like other people. Some are nice, some are cruel. Some work hard, some steal. That thief wasn't even from around here. Don't you remember what the officer said? He knew right off that a local guy wasn't responsible."

"But if you let guys like JD hang around here, people aren't going to feel safe coming to the store. How many customers do you think we've lost because of him or guys like him hanging around?"

Andrea looked down. "I know. I've thought about that. I don't always feel safe bringing Amy down here." She looked back in his eyes. "But Rick, Art sees something in JD, and I really think Art's going to make it now. You don't have to do anything with him. When I saw JD last night I told him this would just be for today, because I'm here. That he'd have to wait for Art to get better before he could start coming around during the week."

Rick was relieved to hear that.

There was a brief pause. "So, are you still mad?"

"No, I'm all right. I don't know what it is, but the guy just gives me the creeps. But I understand your thinking. And this really is Art's place, not mine."

Andrea smiled at him. How could he stay mad at her?

The rest of the day they stayed extremely busy. They had even more sales than the first Saturday after Thanksgiving. And of course, the constant topic at the counter had been Art's miraculous recovery yesterday from the brink of death.

To hear the reaction of the customers in the store, you'd think Art had risen from the dead then walked on water. *Praise the Lord. Thank you, Jesus. Hallelujah, Jesus.* Over and over again. He let Andrea do all the talking. He just provided head nods and smiles. Several congratulated Rick as if he'd played some kind of role. He was glad to hear that Andrea's version of the story contained no hype or exaggeration. He hated when people did that.

Rick had to admit, though, it really was a great story, and it challenged his mind in a good way each time she retold it. But after a day of it, Rick was ready to retire the subject.

Now it was almost quitting time, and the store was empty. What Rick had enjoyed most about the day was all the time he got to spend with Andrea. He couldn't put his finger on it, but she seemed to treat him differently since their talk this morning. Nothing close to romantic interest, as far as he could tell. But there was a certain warmth in her tone and eyes. In those moments between customers, they talked and chatted not unlike a couple on a first date. Short get-to-know-you conversations.

In the last conversation, which, like all the others, had been interrupted by a customer, she started to open up about Amy's father a little. Rick didn't want to lose the momentum. She came back to the counter after cleaning out the coffeepot. "So, Andrea, I know we've got to start wrapping up, but you were talking about Amy's father a few minutes ago—I think you said his name was Greg—and what happened there. Did you want to finish what you were saying, or am I being too nosy?"

"You're not being nosy. There's really not a whole lot more to say. The whole thing is like some sad cliché, the same story that's happened to a thousand high school girls."

"Not ever being a high school girl," Rick said, "afraid I don't know any of the sad clichés."

"You know, shy girl falls in love with the popular guy, doesn't get that he's popular for all the wrong reasons. She gets talked into doing way more than she feels comfortable doing. All kinds of promises exchanged about how much they love each other, will always be together. She gets pregnant. He's not ready to be a parent. Then she finds out what a loser he really is. All he offered was to pay for the abortion. We broke up. I left town and came down here to start over. End of story."

"So he's never helped you out?"

"Not a dime, and I don't want it. I turned to God through the crisis and my whole life got turned around. It's been real hard on us financially. Real hard. But I wouldn't want him involved in Amy's life. He's never tried to contact us, and that's just fine with me."

Rick tried not to show any reaction on his face, but he was aware of how happy he was to hear all this. And also aware of how foolish it was to think it mattered.

35

Over the next few days, Art's condition at Shands continued to stabilize.

At just before 3:00 p.m. on Tuesday, Rick was hanging up the phone after talking a few minutes with his mom. She'd said they were pulling Art out of the induced coma. He was supposed to wake up soon. She'd asked Rick if he wouldn't mind asking folks who came into the store to pray that he would. And that, when he did, he would still be Art.

At the moment, Rick's attention was on a newspaper headline. He couldn't believe what it said.

JOHN LENNON SHOT DEAD

Someone had brought the paper in to show him. Everyone who came in the store was talking about it. It had happened last night in New York City, right outside the entrance to the Dakota, an upscale apartment building where Lennon lived. Some crazy guy named Chapman had been waiting there and, according to witnesses, just stepped out and shot him four or five times in the back. Then he sat down on the sidewalk, waiting for the police to show up and arrest him.

It was hard to fathom. John Lennon dead. One customer said the story had spread like wildfire all over the world. Since arriving in Florida, Rick had completely lost touch with the news, but he didn't mind. It had been nice not to hear the constant drumbeat about hostages and the election.

But now Rick wished he had a television or a radio to hear the latest on the story. The brass bell rang. He looked up. It was Andrea. There was a chill in the air. She took off her coat and hung it on the rack.

"You hear about John Lennon?" she asked.

"I was just reading about it. It's crazy. Why would someone shoot John Lennon?"

"They're saying the guy might be insane." She put her purse under the counter. "They've got the television on at the diner, been covering it all morning. You should see the people, huge crowds gathering in New York and other cities. People are crying, bringing flowers."

"Lennon's huge," Rick said. "I mean . . . we're talking the Beatles."

"I can't believe he's dead. I've been hoping someday they might get back together."

"You like the Beatles?"

"Of course I like the Beatles. Well, some of their stuff, anyway."

"Let me guess, the early years? 'I Want to Hold Your Hand.' 'She Loves You' . . ."

"Yeah, yeah, yeah," she said, half-singing. "All the early sixties stuff. I wasn't that into them when all the drug and Eastern religion stuff started coming out."

"We got into all that too," said Rick. "My friends and I used to sit around and read the lyrics on the cover, trying to figure out the secret meanings."

"Here's the secret," she said. "They were stoned out of their minds. C'mon, joo-joo eyeballs? Toe-jam football? Not exactly their best work."

Rick laughed.

The Christmas cassette ended. She got up to change it. "I think they got a kick out of all the morons who hung on every word they said. They probably just tossed things in there to play with their heads."

"So I'm a moron?"

"Not you, Rick. I'm talking about the other morons."

Rick smiled. He was enjoying this. "So what other songs were your favorites?"

"I don't know. 'Yesterday' is incredible. I think people will be singing that fifty years from now. Oh, 'And I Love Her.' I love that song. I like 'Blackbird' . . . 'The Long and Winding Road.' And I love 'The Fool on the Hill.'"

"You don't love the Beatles, you love Paul McCartney," Rick said.

"Maybe I do then. You don't think someone's going to try to kill him next, do you?"

"I don't know. I don't think so." Rick shook his head. The shooting made no sense. But he was surprised and happy to learn Andrea liked the Beatles. The little bell rang. It was the surfer, Mack, and two of his friends.

"Dude," he said. "You hear they shot Lennon?"

▲

Leanne couldn't help it; she was nervous. Art had been off heavy sedation for almost two hours now. Over the last few days, the nurses had helped her understand the different monitors. His numbers all seemed to be okay. His blood pressure had remained steady ever since Charlie had prayed.

She got out of her chair and walked to his bed, took his hand. All she'd had since the day after Thanksgiving was that one glorious conversation before his surgery.

She wanted more, years more. *Lord, please let him wake up.*

One of the machines beeped loudly, startling her. She didn't know which one it was, but it did that every so often. She was told it was nothing to worry about.

"Leanne?"

Her eyes darted from the machine to Art's face. "I'm here, Art." *He knows my name.* She squeezed his hand. "You feel that?"

"Yes." He squeezed back.. "Is it over?"

"Is what over?"

"The surgery."

"Goodness, yes. Five days ago." *He's remembering things.*

"Five days. What day is it?"

"Tuesday. They had to keep you under till the swelling from the surgery went down. I'm so glad you're awake. I've missed you so much." She laid her head gently on his chest and cried. She felt his hand patting her head.

"Have I missed Christmas?" he asked.

She lifted her head. "No, darlin'. Still got two more weeks."

"Where are we?"

"Still at Shands in Gainesville. But the doctors said if you woke up today and things looked good, they might drive you back to Seabreeze tomorrow."

"Home?"

"Not yet. Just back to our hospital. They've got to keep a close eye on you for at least another week or so. Run a bunch more tests to see if the surgery affected anything they weren't planning on."

"Like what?"

"The doctor said whenever they fiddle with the brain, there's no telling what might happen. They were preparing me for the possibility that you wouldn't even know who I was."

Art smiled. "Leanne, do you remember when we ate eggs Benedict made with crabmeat in that outdoor courtyard in Charleston?"

"That little café off Meeting Street," she said.

"The coffee was almost as good as yours," he said. "Almost."

"Our fifth wedding anniversary trip."

"The azaleas blooming all around us, remember? The dogwoods?"

"And that jasmine."

"Especially at night, the smell. Remember that smell?"

She remembered it all. And so did he. Thank you, Lord. So did he.

"Leanne," he said. "I would never forget you. I'd forget who I am before I'd forget you."

36

Rick locked the front door to the store. Andrea waited for him on the sidewalk. It had been a good day. Best sales day so far. Best conversations with Andrea so far.

It was time to try again.

He walked up the steps. "Going to pick up Amy?"

She nodded. "I can't believe I've got to go home and fix dinner. I'm so tired."

Perfect. Like she was lobbing a softball right to him. "I am too. Tell you what, why don't you let me help? They've got these places, just like the diner, except these places fix dinners. We don't have to do a thing, just show up."

"I don't think so, Rick. I've got to get Amy."

"What, you thought I meant we'd leave her out? These places feed kids too." Rick could see it in her eyes. She wasn't buying it.

"I don't think so."

"You sure? You said you were tired."

"I am." She was backing up.

"Don't have to go anywhere fancy. We could go to HoJo's, where I'm staying. They serve these terrible clam dinners, but the ice cream is delicious."

"I'm not looking for, I mean . . . I don't want Amy to get the wrong impression."

You mean, you don't want me to get the wrong impression. "We could get her a sitter." Now, he was begging.

"Thanks, Rick. Maybe another time."

"All right. See you tomorrow."

She smiled, waved, turned and headed for her car.

What was he thinking? *Maybe another time.* She wasn't interested. Not now. Not that way. And he wasn't interested in being humiliated again.

She didn't have to worry. There wouldn't be another time.

Andrea sighed heavily. She put on her seat belt, turned on the car, and looked in the rearview mirror. Rick was getting into his car. She waited a moment as he turned it on, pulled out onto the road, and passed her by.

She waved. He just looked straight ahead.

She had hurt him this time, she could feel it, see it in his eyes. But what else could she do? They still seemed worlds apart, on everything that mattered most to her. She couldn't think of a way to talk about it that wouldn't come off sounding like she thought she was better than he was; "holier than thou," as they say.

But she couldn't afford to feel what she was starting to feel for him. She couldn't allow herself to become just the latest in his long line of conquests. She pulled out onto the road and drove a few blocks before she realized she was heading in the wrong direction. That's right, she had to pick up Amy.

Amy . . . she was more than half the reason Andrea knew she had to keep putting Rick off. She had resolved some time ago that she wouldn't put Amy through a long line of boyfriends and fake daddies just to satisfy her craving for love and a little romance. She'd tried that the first two years after Amy had been born.

She was so glad Amy was too young to remember.

But Andrea would never let herself forget.

37

It was Wednesday afternoon, a little after 3:00 p.m. Rick's mom had called at noon, the happiest he'd heard her since this whole thing with Art had begun. The doctors had given the green light to transfer him back to the smaller ICU in Seabreeze. She said they'd be on the road around 1:00 p.m. Rick looked at his watch. That meant they'd be arriving in an hour or two.

She was even more excited that Art was awake and talking again. As far as she could tell, there had been no permanent brain damage. At least in terms of his speech, memory, and personality. She said all kinds of other things could pop up down the road.

The telephone rang. He walked toward the front counter and picked it up. "The Book Nook, Rick speaking."

"Hi, Rick, it's Andrea."

"Hey, Andrea."

"Guess you heard about your mom and Art coming into town."

"Should be here in an hour or two would be my guess."

"That's why I'm calling. Your mom asked if I could stop by the house and get a short list of things for her and bring them out to the hospital after the store closes. But I thought

I'd skip coming in today, unless you're real busy, and go by the house now. Maybe I could spruce things up a little, see if she needs any laundry done."

"That's very kind of you, Andrea. I'm sure she'll appreciate it. Things are fine here. Had a big rush during lunch, but it's been one or two at a time since then."

"Okay, good." She hesitated a few moments.

"Anything else?" he asked.

"No, guess I'll see you tomorrow then."

"All right, see you then." He hung up.

No sense pretending, trying to keep the conversation alive. He decided to busy himself with a little project he'd started over the last few days. He'd remembered how to set up the books for a very small company from a school project he'd done years ago. He'd been keeping Art's whacked-out system running but started a whole new setup for him to try once he felt up to it. It was so simple, a monkey could maintain it.

He was less certain you could teach an old monkey new tricks.

———————▲———————

Art was sound asleep. But that was okay. He was just asleep. The doctor had given him a mild sedative for the ride home. He assured Leanne that Art should wake right up when it wore off. He was back in the same ICU room in Seabreeze he'd been in before they'd left for Shands. Holly had gotten him all squared away. Dr. Halper had already been in to make sure all his numbers were good and everything was working as it should.

He still suggested that after Art woke up to keep him calm, keep the noise to a minimum. But he felt they could let in some light from the window. Just the sliver coming in now seemed as bright as the sunrise compared to what it had been.

Holly poked her head in the doorway. "Got a visitor. A friend named Andrea. She's in the waiting room."

"Thanks, dear. I'll be right there." Leanne had been expecting this. Andrea had called from the house about a half hour ago, asking if she could have a private chat with her after she dropped off the things she brought from the house. Leanne wondered what to expect, hoped nothing sour had happened between Andrea and Rick down at the store.

"Hello?" Leanne said, peeking her head in the waiting room door. She was glad to find it empty except for Andrea.

"Leanne?" Andrea rushed toward her and gave her a big hug. When she pulled back, her eyes were full of tears. "I've missed you so much, and I've been so worried about Art, about the both of you."

"I've missed you too, Andrea. But we're doing okay, really." Leanne pulled a tissue from a Kleenex box on the corner table and gave it to her. "Looks like God's going to let me keep Art a while longer."

"I'm so glad. Is he awake yet?"

"No, but he should be soon."

"Okay, then I won't keep you." She backed up and sat in a chair. "Oh, here are the things you asked for."

Leanne took the bag and sat beside her. She didn't want to hurry her, but she really wanted to be there when Art woke up. "Thanks so much for doing that . . . so what's up?"

"This is going to be a strange conversation for me. I've been trying to think about the best way to say it."

"Andrea, don't be nervous. You can talk to me. I may be much older, but we're also friends."

"Leanne, you've been the best friend to me. Better than anyone." She inhaled deeply. "It's about Rick. I'm so confused." She dabbed her eyes.

"What's the matter?"

"He's asked me out to dinner twice since we've been working together."

"Oh." Leanne wasn't really surprised to hear this. "What did you say?"

"No . . . both times. As gently as I could."

Leanne expected this too. "Did Rick respond badly?"

"No, but I could see he was hurt, and I don't want to hurt him."

"I can't see him staying hurt for too long. He's planning on heading back to Charlotte soon, right?"

"That's one thing on my list of reasons for saying no. I can't go out with someone casually. I won't do that to Amy, even if I wanted to."

Leanne asked, "Do you want to? Is that why you're confused?"

"See? You always know what I'm thinking." The tears came again. She pushed some back, wiped away others. "The first time I said no, it was easy. Last night . . . I really wanted to say yes. But it's so wrong. *He* is so wrong for me in so many ways." She looked up into Leanne's eyes. "I'm sorry, I shouldn't have said that. He's your son."

"Don't apologize, Andrea. I agree with you."

"You do?"

"I love Rick, but . . . so far I haven't seen any signs that he's ready to settle down. And you need that."

"I do. I need a guy who doesn't want to just date me. Unless he's serious about wanting to get to know me, and because he . . ."

"Wants to marry you?"

"Yes."

"You don't need to apologize for that. I think that's God's will for you at this point in your life. You don't want to do that to Amy, parading this guy and that guy in front of her, just so you can have fun."

"I don't. I *really* don't."

"Of course, you don't. There's nothing wrong with that."

"And I'm also concerned about . . . his lack of faith. I want a man who is serious about the Lord. Do you know where he's at with God?"

Leanne knew this was coming. "I wish I did, Andrea. I've been praying for him for years. So has Art. He seemed to have an experience with God, shortly after I did. But he was much younger then, his first year of junior high, I think. But he started pulling away from me after Art and I got together. About the same time, he started pulling away from God too. To be honest, that's been my biggest concern for him working down at the store. How he'd react being totally surrounded by Christians every day. I just decided God must know what he's doing, because I had no one else to call who could also handle the money side of things."

"Well, I don't know what God's doing in Rick's heart," Andrea said. "He does seem to have changed some since the first day. He's a little . . . softer, I guess. Easier to talk to. But I'd need to know he's got a lot more than that going on before I'd feel okay starting a relationship with him."

"I understand. I'm right there with you on this."

Andrea looked off to the side. "I know Amy is totally smitten with him."

"Really?" Leanne asked.

Andrea nodded. "Both times she's been at the store, he's the only thing she talks about the rest of the night. But I can't let that matter. I don't want her getting hurt."

Leanne put her hand on Andrea's shoulder. "It's okay, Andrea. Amy has to come first. You're just being a good mom. We'll just have to give it to God and pray that he does some kind of major surgery on Rick's heart. That's the real problem. What he needs most is out of your reach . . . and mine."

———— ▲ ————

Rick locked up the store for the night, an hour past the normal time. He'd gotten sucked into that bookkeeping project for Art. As he climbed the cement steps, he heard someone talking around the rear corner of the building. He instantly knew who it was, that stupid JD talking to himself again. He was arguing with someone named Taylor about which charity they should mooch off tonight.

Rick had enough.

He walked around the corner, saw JD on all fours about to climb back into his box. "Yo, JD," Rick yelled.

JD looked at him, his face instantly gripped with fear. He crawled the rest of the way inside his box.

"Go ahead and hide," Rick yelled. "But I know you can hear me. I want you off this property by morning or I'm calling the cops. I know Andrea gave you a McMuffin on Saturday, and Art's supposed to be on the mend. Maybe they'll let you come back later. But while I'm here, I want you gone. When I come back tomorrow morning, if you're still here, I'll have you arrested. You got that?" Rick waited for an answer.

"I know you heard me," he said and headed toward his car.

38

The next morning, Rick pulled up to his parking spot next to the Book Nook. He set his coffee on the little wall bordering the steps and walked to the rear of the building. The big box was still there. He walked up to it and started banging on the side. "You in there, JD?"

He waited. No answer.

He banged on it again. "JD?" He lifted up one side. It was empty. He wished they had a dumpster so he could get rid of it altogether. Maybe later he'd call the city, see if they could do something. He walked back to the sidewalk, grabbed his coffee, and opened the store.

The rest of the day went as expected. By now, Rick had settled into a predictable routine. He still couldn't tell someone which book to read, but he'd gotten a pretty good handle on the rest of the inventory, including the record albums. He knew where most things were, what aisle, what shelf. Of course, he realized this was no great achievement. It was the expectation of every boss who'd ever hired a high school kid to work retail, given the same amount of time.

But Rick had to admit, he liked it. Liked the pace, liked the routine. Even the customers, somehow they had become only half as annoying. On the whole, they were a pleasant lot.

Even the ones who brought things back never complained. If anything, they blamed themselves for picking the wrong thing and taking up his time running it back through the register. Most felt guilty enough to go back in the store and buy something else that cost just as much.

And every single one, without fail, asked about Art and his mom. *How's Art doing? What's the latest? How's Leanne holding up? Tell them we're still praying.* And every single one made a separate point to talk about how much they loved coming into the store, how wonderful Art and his mom were.

At the moment, Rick was sitting in the back office, trying to finish up that bookkeeping project. Andrea had come in around 2:45. Their conversation at the counter had seemed a bit strained, at least for him. She seemed fine, like there wasn't a problem. Pretty as ever. Nice as ever. Rick tried to pretend he was fine. Kept it light. But all the while there was this pressure building inside him. He just wanted to know: *Why won't you go out with me? Why won't you give me a chance?*

There was no way he'd say it.

So when the store traffic quieted down, he'd told her he should head back to the office, work on this project. For a moment, he'd thought she seemed disappointed. Probably just his imagination.

"Hey, Rick."

He looked up. Andrea's head poked through the doorway. "Quitting time. I'm going to start shutting things down, if that's all right. Got to go pick up Amy."

"No, that's fine," he said.

"Your mother called from the hospital. Guess you didn't hear it."

"Is everything all right?"

"Yeah, she said Art's had a good day. She's still trying to get used to him wearing a turban."

"A turban?"

"His head, it's all bandaged up."

"Oh, right."

"I asked if she wanted me to come get you. She said she didn't want to interrupt you but wondered if you'd call back before you left."

"Sure. You have a good night," Rick said.

"You too."

"And say hi to Amy for me."

"I will."

As soon as she'd left, Rick realized something. He hadn't asked about Amy for Andrea's sake, trying to impress her. It came out on its own.

But Rick hated kids, didn't he? It was almost a policy.

39

This was going to be strange.

Rick drove his Celica to a part of town he hadn't seen in over ten years. On purpose. He remembered feeling the sensation of fleeing the last time he'd been here.

Just before leaving the store, he had called his mom back. She'd asked him for a favor. She knew it was a big one and apologized for even asking. Would he stop by her house— his old house—to pick up some prayer journal Andrea had forgotten yesterday and bring it out to the hospital?

He was in the neighborhood now, just a few blocks away. Nothing had changed. Except all the trees were bigger. It was an older section of town, the homes all built shortly after World War II. Rick thought they certainly knew how to build things in those days. Seabreeze had been hit by at least a half dozen big hurricanes since then, but every house still stood strong. Most were in pretty good shape. He found himself admiring the homes, the manicured yards, the flower boxes in the windows. He waved at a number of middle-aged and elderly people as he drove by. He wondered how many might be older, balder, grayer versions of people he'd known in his teens.

He turned right onto his old street, Waverly Road. His eyes

instantly veered to the left, to the fifth house. Right where it was supposed to be. He pulled into the driveway, stopped the car just a few yards in. He sat there a while to take it in.

Why had he hated this place?

It might be the cutest house in a neighborhood of bunga-lows. That's what they built back then. Art hadn't changed a thing. Even kept the same shade of yellow. The house sat comfortably on the left side of the driveway, surrounded by large shady oaks, moss hanging down from every limb. It had this high-pitched gable roof with dark green shingles. A charming little dormer poked out, facing the street. A porch stretched across the front. The whole thing trimmed in white. The driveway went straight back to a freestanding garage, a small replica of the house itself.

He got out of the car and walked toward the front door. Four steps led up to the porch. On opposite ends of each step sat large clay pots, the flowers shriveled from last week's freeze. He found the front door key under the second pot on the left. Right where his mom said. He opened the door and stepped inside.

My, Rick thought. Nothing had changed. All these years. Except the sofa and recliner. But even they were the same color. There was the stone fireplace in the corner. Art's old wooden rocker off to the side. He used to hate what he saw in here. Embarrassed at how small it was. He'd never invite in friends from high school. Most of the time when he'd catch a ride, he'd have them drop him off at the corner. All his friends lived in modern subdivisions, miles from here. Closer to the beach. In ranch-style houses with central heat and air. More than half had pools.

He walked through the living room all decorated with Christmas colors and knickknacks. Santas and snowmen sitting on every shelf. It *was* small, so was the dining area. He looked at the kitchen. His condo kitchen was bigger than this. But none of it seemed to matter now. Instead of feeling small, it felt . . . cozy. That was the charm of a bungalow. Nice little home with nice little rooms. No wasted space. Was it a memory or did he smell coffee? His mom always made the best coffee.

He looked over at the little dinette set, where he'd eaten ten thousand bowls of cereal.

That's right, the prayer journal. Mom said it was in her bedroom, next to the nightstand or on her chest of drawers. He walked back through the living room and into the small hallway connecting the two bedrooms, the one bath in between. He flicked on the light and was almost startled by the dozens of picture frames hanging in the hallway.

He took a few minutes to study them. Art or his mom, or the both of them, were in every one. They all seemed to have been taken since Rick had left. He wasn't in a single one. But then, why would he be? There were pictures of them at the store. Gardening in the backyard. In St. Augustine. At Disney World. Standing next to Niagara Falls. *When did they go there?* On a big fishing boat; Art was helping his mom hold up a three-foot-long fish. There were several pictures of them with Father Charlie and another woman. Rick supposed his wife.

Rick couldn't help but notice how happy they were. His eyes zeroed in on his mother's face, beaming in every shot. He was about to turn, head into their bedroom, when one picture caught his eye. It was a picture of them in the living room, standing in front of the Christmas tree. Had to be taken the past year or two. Art stared ahead at the camera, smiling away. But his mom was looking sideways at Art. She was smiling, but she had another look on her face. Rick knew what it was.

The look of a woman in love. Art really had made his mother happy. All these years. And he had taken really good care of her.

Rick stepped into their bedroom, grateful that Art seemed to be pulling through this ordeal. He looked to the far side of the bed. There was a little black book, too small to be a Bible. He walked around the bed and picked it up. As he flipped it open, he instantly recognized his mother's handwriting.

Mission accomplished. He closed the book and headed for the door. He stopped in the hallway, aware of a strong curiosity to open the journal and read a few pages. Just a few. *No, you can't do that. That's like reading someone's diary.* He walked a few more steps and stopped. *Just a look, what could it hurt?* He opened it from the back, flipped till he came to the last entry.

At the top, she'd written "Thanksgiving Day, 1980." The day before Art had collapsed.

Thank you, Lord for a wonderful day. Thank you for giving up your life for me. Thank you for Art, for giving me such a wonderful man. Thank you for giving us so many good friends. Thanks for helping us get the store all decorated yesterday. Thank you for the store itself, for using it to provide all our needs and allowing us to be a blessing to others.

Thank you for my wonderful son, Rick. Be with him today. Open the eyes of his heart, Lord. I pray he would know you and know all that you have done for him. I pray I'd be able to talk with him today. Please have him call or let him be there when I do . . .

Thank you for my wonderful son, Rick?
How had he been a wonderful son to her? Rick felt a ripple

of guilt as he realized where his head had been on Thanksgiving Day. For starters, he'd woken up with a hangover. He'd watched the end of the Macy's Thanksgiving Parade in his pj's, then eaten his Thanksgiving dinner with some friends. He'd hardly thought of his mom, except to dread the inevitable phone call with her that day.

He closed the journal. Just before he entered the living room, another surge of curiosity came over him. His old room. The door was half open. He walked in, flicked on the light switch. It was remarkable. Like the day he'd left it, everything the same. Even the surf posters thumbtacked to the walls. The big Atlanta Braves pennant over his bed. His bedspread was the same, light green with little cottony puffs. He used to pull them apart when he talked on the phone. Sitting on the nightstand was the same phone, the old rotary kind.

He walked to his dresser, a dark wooden thing, probably an antique. If not then, certainly now. He wondered what was inside. He yanked on the knobs of the top drawer. One side came out first, the other side stuck, same as ever. He pushed it back and pulled harder on the weak side till the drawer broke free.

What he saw surprised him. It was filled with greeting cards. He grabbed a small handful and set them on top of the dresser. They looked familiar. As soon as he opened the first one, he knew why. They were cards he'd sent his mom over the years. On her birthday, Mother's Day, her and Art's anniversary. After opening a few, he put them all back. He knew there was nothing to read. He'd never written a single note in a single card. Just signed them "Rick." Once in a while, "Love, Rick."

He'd never spent more than a few moments picking out a card. Sometimes he wouldn't even read what the card said. Just signed it. Sometimes he'd forget to mail it. Then send it days later.

Thank you for my wonderful son, Rick.

He couldn't believe she'd saved every single one. He closed the drawer, but it stuck as usual. As he shoved it harder, a small wooden box sitting inside the drawer slid forward. He opened the drawer the rest of the way, lifted the box, and set it on the dresser. Looked like the kind of box you put keepsakes in. But it wasn't his. He'd never seen it before.

He wondered what was inside.

40

Rick lifted the box lid. He was immediately disappointed.

Even though he didn't recognize the box, he still expected to find things about him inside. Maybe things his mother had saved through the years, little gifts he'd given her that he'd forgotten about. Instead, he saw a handful of cards paper-clipped to a thin stack of papers. Next to it, a set of keys. He picked the keys up; a dozen of them were hooked to a rusty ring. The biggest was definitely to a car. He turned and held it up to the light.

"Toyota," he mumbled aloud. It was etched in the plastic, almost rubbed off. Art and his mom drove a Buick, as he recalled. Didn't remember them ever owning a Toyota. He tossed it back in the box and took out the papers.

"What?" he said as his eyes caught a few words. *This can't be right*. He pulled the paper clip off and walked over to the bed, where the light was brighter.

"How is this possible?" he said, setting all but the first item on the bed. *What is this doing here?* It was an old Social Security card, wrinkled and yellowed at the edges. He read the name below the nine-digit number:

James Michael Denton

That was his father's name. It was his father's card!

He set it down and grabbed the second card in the stack. A library card, just as old, bearing the County Seal of Cobb County, Georgia. And the name:

James Denton

Is that where his father had gone? Cobb County, Georgia? Is that where he'd been all these years? He was pretty sure Cobb County was somewhere near Atlanta. But why is it here? he thought, eyeing the card again.

He set it down and reached for one of the papers. It was almost tissue thin, so he unfolded it carefully. He felt his stomach turn. It was his father's birth certificate. There was his full name—James Michael Denton. And his birth date. The hospital in Dayton, Ohio, where he was born. It wasn't a copy; it had a raised seal.

Rick's heart began to race, one step ahead of a thought that began to form. Why would original cards and papers like this be in this box, in this room . . . in this house? It could only mean one thing. Tears welled up in his eyes as the realization struck home.

His father was dead.

What else could it be? He hadn't talked with his mom about his father for years, but the last time he had, she'd said she hadn't heard from him since that first year he'd left. These were the kinds of documents you keep in a safe place in your own home, or a safe-deposit box. Not at your ex-wife's house. He must have died, and some lawyer had sent his important documents to her.

He wiped his eyes and sat up straight. Now he was getting angry. Why hadn't she told him? He had a right to know. He wondered when it had happened. There must be a death certificate in here somewhere. He started leafing through the other documents but couldn't find one. Just a letter to his father from a life insurance company saying his policy had expired, and a car insurance document for a 1971 Toyota Corolla. Rick looked at the date. Also expired. But no death certificate.

He had started gathering everything back together when he noticed what looked like a driver's license at the bottom of the stack of cards. He pulled it out and instantly saw his father's name: James Michael Denton. Then looked at his picture. It was like looking at the face of a stranger. He tried to make the connection between this image and his childhood memories, but he could barely see it. The man was so much older, his hair mostly gray on the sides, deep shadows under his eyes. He wasn't smiling; his mouth hung slightly open.

Rick looked at the issue date—almost four years ago. The license was from the state of Georgia as well. So . . . he had died sometime in the last four years. He looked back at his father's picture. He didn't look well; you could see it in his eyes. *What happened to you?* Sadness pushed his anger aside. He stood up, then paper-clipped everything together, except the license. He wanted to keep it to show it to his mom when he confronted her.

He set everything back in the wooden box, slipped the box back inside the drawer. He walked out into the hall, then turned around and flipped the light switch off in his bedroom. He wished he'd never gone in there. But then, maybe he was supposed to. How else would he have found out his father had died? Didn't seem like his mom had any intention of telling him.

As he walked across the short hallway, he reached for the hall light switch, then froze in his tracks.

"What? No."

The light was much brighter here. He lifted the driver's license up to catch a better angle. *It can't be. No, it can't be.*

He shook his head, refusing to accept what first his eyes and now his mind were telling him. He stared again at the face of his father. Here in the light of the hallway, it was coming clearly into focus.

Oh, how he wished he was wrong.

Though he couldn't make any connection to childhood memories in his father's face, it did connect with someone he had seen very recently. Several times, in fact, over the last two weeks. It meant his father was not dead, but this thought brought no relief.

He looked at the picture again and again. And as he did, he pictured the man he had in mind. There could be no mistake.

It was him.

Add several more years to the face. Make the hair much grayer and much longer. Add in a long, matted beard. Put on a dirty, wrinkled raincoat.

The man in the driver's license—his father—was Columbo. The homeless guy hanging around the Book Nook.

Rick read the name again . . . James Michael Denton.

James Denton.

JD.

JD was Rick's father.

41

Art was sitting up. And he was eating.

Leanne was beside herself.

He was still weak, still hooked up to all these machines, but Dr. Halper had just left an hour ago. He'd pulled Leanne off to the side and said he was increasingly hopeful Art was going to make it. Those were the strongest words he'd used so far. And he was smiling. He thought Art was ready to start eating for himself. If it went well, he'd take him off the IV feeding tube. Then he wanted to slowly ease Art into a series of tests to determine if there had been any collateral damage from the surgery.

"How is it, Art?" She had just fed him a mouthful of macaroni and cheese.

He chewed and nodded his head.

"Good?"

He smiled, kept chewing.

His head was still wrapped in bandages. There was some bruising around his eyes. His face sagged a bit from all the weight loss. But to her, he looked wonderful. Less than a week ago she thought she'd be spending this Christmas as a widow. She gave him another spoonful.

He chewed some more. A puzzled look crossed his face.

"This is macaroni and cheese?" he said quietly after swallowing. "I'm not tasting the cheese."

"Well, it's hospital food. Here, have some more."

He ate another four or five spoonfuls, then said, "You taste it, hon. See what you think. I'm glad to be eating something real, but . . . I still don't taste any cheese."

Leanne took a spoonful. Maybe she had been in a hospital environment too long, but it didn't taste too bad to her. "It's not as good as mine, but I definitely taste the cheese. Here, try another bite."

He ate several more spoonfuls. "Nope, just tastes like squishy noodles."

"Well, here, let's try the Jell-O."

After several spoonfuls of lime Jell-O, Art shook his head. "I don't taste anything."

Leanne took a bite. To her, it tasted good enough to finish the whole cup. "I can taste it."

"Really?" he said. "Maybe the meds are messing with my taste buds."

"Maybe." Of course, she didn't know. "How's your stomach feel?"

"Fine."

"Then just see if you can eat it all, and we'll talk to Dr. Halper tomorrow about the taste thing. Right now, the goal is to get you off the feeding tube."

"I'm all for that, so let's eat."

She gave him a few more spoonfuls of Jell-O.

"I could get used to this," he said, smiling, referring to being hand fed.

She loved it when he smiled. To be able to see it again, hear his voice again. That's what mattered. Not something like this taste problem. Still, she hoped it wasn't something permanent. Art loved food so much, and she loved making it for him.

As he finished up the Jell-O, she wondered what other post-surgery surprises lay in store.

———▲———

Rick fled the house as the shock of the news sunk in. He had to get out of there but wasn't sure where to go. He hopped into his car and drove off. Tears streamed down his face. It didn't make sense. How could it be true? How could this crazed, homeless guy be his father? Images from the last two weeks began to flood his mind.

The disgusting first impression of JD at the store that first day, begging for an Egg McMuffin.

Watching him cross the street by the Davis Brothers Toy Store that night, arms flailing about as he argued with some imaginary friend.

JD walking around the corner, the morning after the big freeze, all wrapped in a blanket.

The terror on his face at the park, right after the robbery, when Rick found him and tackled him to the ground. My gosh, Rick thought . . . I tackled my father. And he remembered how much he wanted to punch JD out just then.

Then yesterday, watching this pathetic little man crawling back into his stupid box, trying to run from Rick as Rick yelled at him to get off the property.

An image of a recent conversation with Andrea came to mind as she explained to Rick why she was being kind to JD. And Rick's reply: *"Andrea, it's just . . . the guy is homeless. He smells. He lives in a box. He talks to himself."*

Rick smacked the dashboard. How could JD be his father?

He looked up, realized he had stopped at a stop sign a few miles from the old house. He didn't recall making a single turn getting here, but he recognized the spot. It was like a more rational part of his mind had involuntarily taken over. If he turned right here, the road would lead to Riverside

Drive, another road that ran right along the river. Then left a few more blocks and he'd be at a place he used to always run to when he'd get angry or upset. It was a public dock, with a wooden fishing pier that stuck out fifty yards into the river. No one ever used it since they'd built better facilities near the bridge.

He wondered if it was still there.

———— ▲ ————

It was just after 7:00 p.m., totally dark now.

But the dock and fishing pier were still here. They'd removed the big light at the end of the pier, but the moon was out at three-quarters strength, plenty of light to find his way. He stepped carefully across the boards, which creaked and cracked much louder than he recalled; he hoped his leg wouldn't fall through.

The old wooden bench was still there, sagging a bit in the middle. Rick felt like standing anyway. He leaned against the rail. A gentle breeze blew against his face, with just enough chill to feel refreshing. It was so peaceful and calm. Tiny river waves slapped against the wooden pilings. Across the river, the black silhouette of hundreds of palm trees rose up to meet the deep blue sky. The dock was, perhaps, a mile north of all the mansions that lined both sides of the river leading back into town. Rick was glad the town's progress had slowed in his absence, leaving this place alone.

He needed this place to be here. Just as it was.

"God, I don't understand," he prayed out loud. But quietly. How could things turn out this way? How could the man he'd loved and cherished as a young boy and, if anything, had grown to love even more in the years since, have turned out like this?

He realized he'd allowed his memories of his father to grow into almost mythical status. Rick's fantasy included his father showing up one day in the future—handsome, successful, perhaps the CEO of a large corporation—wanting to reconnect with Rick. He figured his father would have some explanation for the years of silence, but Rick had already decided he didn't care about his reasons. He just wanted to be with him again.

And when his father came, he would be impressed with how much Rick had achieved on his own. Then together, they'd make up for lost time, maybe sail the Caribbean for a year getting caught up, maybe after that go into business together.

"You idiot," he said. "It's JD. That's who you've been waiting for."

He jumped, startled by a noise at the other end of the pier. He shook his head and smiled. A pelican had arrived in time to hear his confession. "You sure you wanna hear this, old fella?" The pelican flew off. "Don't blame you."

Then he cried for a while. A few more thoughts, more feelings and mental pictures. Dissolving one by one.

A brief funeral for the death of a dream.

A sharp, chilly gust came across the river. He was grateful. He straightened up, wishing at that moment that guys still used handkerchiefs. He wiped his tears away, first with his hands, then his sleeve. New thoughts began to form. But now his heart was calm, open to hear them. He'd had it all wrong from the start.

All of it.

About his mom, about Art.

Especially Art.

Certain facts about how JD's—his father's—cards and papers had made their way into that little wooden box began to gel. Andrea had said Art had been feeding JD those Egg McMuffins for just over a year. She said Art had seen something in him worth caring about, that he was reaching out to him.

That meant Andrea didn't know. He didn't know why, but for now, he was glad.

So . . . some time shortly before that, his homeless, schizophrenic father had wandered into town. And at some point, Art and Leanne had found out about it. With his dad's mental state so deteriorated, it couldn't have been much of a reunion. But they had decided to help him, if they could. From what Andrea had said about Art, Rick could imagine Art actually inviting JD to set up his box behind the store.

Rick looked up at the moon and sighed.

Why would Art do that? It made no sense.

Rick had thrown his fantasy father in Art's face for years. The man Art could never replace. The man Art could never measure up to. An image flashed into Rick's mind of the last time Art had invited Rick to go fishing with him. The snook were running. Art stood by his bedside, gently pleading. Rick had his back turned toward him. "Art, would you just stop this? I'm not going fishing with you. You don't think I get what you're trying to do? Just give it up. You're not my father. You're never going to be my father."

He'd been so harsh. Tears rolled down Rick's cheeks as he remembered. He stared out at the water a few minutes, let the quiet scene speak to him; the moon shimmered on the water, like the still small voice of God. Art had known the truth about Rick's father for over a year. But he'd never said a word.

Rick knew how he'd have reacted if he'd been Art. He'd have hated JD, did whatever he could to make his life miserable. He'd have called Rick within hours and let him have it. *"You think your old man's something special, right? The superhero, the white knight who's gonna show up one day and make your life wonderful? Well, guess what? I'm looking at him right now. A stinking, penniless drunk. Hardly even knows who he is. Why don't you drive down here and have a look?"*

It's exactly what Rick would have done. But not Art. Art did just the opposite. Did everything he could to help JD. And he didn't say a word to Rick about it, he let Rick continue to keep his fantasy father intact. And if Art hadn't had that aneurysm, he'd still be doing his best to help JD, and still be allowing Rick to think the worst about him and the best about his father.

Why? Why would Art do this?

Rick looked back at the moon. He knew why.

Art wasn't the man he'd hated all these years. He wasn't even close. Rick had been hearing about who Art really was for the last two weeks. From one customer after another.

And from Andrea.

He closed his eyes and looked down. He remembered the feelings he'd had in his bedroom on that morning years ago, the dark angry feelings toward Art. He could almost feel Art standing there behind him as he lashed out at him with his words. Remembered the long pause, then Art's quiet footsteps leaving his room.

Rick dropped to the deck and began to sob. *Oh Art, I'm so sorry.* He couldn't talk. Just knelt there crying. *God, please forgive me.*

Another funeral of sorts was underway. But this time, not the death of a dream but the death of an entire way of life.

42

Rick wasn't sure how long he'd been out on that dock. He'd lost all sense of time. All he knew as he headed back to his car was that he felt completely different inside. The anger was gone. The frustration, gone. The confusion about what all this meant, gone. For some reason, he didn't feel a need to know and didn't care. It was totally unlike him. What he felt instead was something very close to joy.

He instantly knew what to do.

He got in his car and headed back to the house. He'd been in such a hurry before, he'd left his mother's prayer journal in the living room. He hadn't even locked the door on his way out. He was heading back to take care of both items, but he had a few other things he wanted to pick up before he drove out to the hospital.

At the first intersection, his Christopher Cross cassette ended and self-ejected. The radio kicked in, filling the car with Christmas music. The odd thing was, he didn't change the channel or put in another cassette. He actually sang along. "Sleigh bells ring, are ya listenin', in the lane snow is glistenin'."

He noticed the time: 8:23 p.m. His mother probably thought he'd forgotten all about her. He hadn't eaten any dinner but didn't care. He needed to get out to the hospital.

Within a few minutes, he pulled into the driveway. By now, the whole property was pitch black, the moonlight blocked by the huge umbrella of trees. But he knew the way. He made his way up the steps, turned on a few lights, and gathered the things he'd come back to get.

One of them wasn't in the house. It was out in the garage.

▲

Art was asleep. He had a peaceful look on his face.

So much better than the look on his face all those terrible days right after his aneurysm. Leanne really felt now he was going to get better, that the worst was over. She remembered the conversations she'd had with Dr. Halper, when he'd tried to prepare her for the worst. The percentage of people who died before reaching the hospital. The percentage who died within the first few days after that. The percentage who died during surgery. The percentage who survived surgery but suffered from permanent brain damage.

So far, Art couldn't taste cheese and Jell-O.

She could live with that. Even a few worse things. But he could talk with her, and when he did, he was Art, through and through. She heard a noise behind her and turned. It was Holly.

"Hey, Leanne, a young man is in the waiting room. Haven't seen him before, but he said he's your son Rick."

"Oh Rick, I almost forgot. I asked him if he could pick up something I left at the house. I'll be right there."

"Well, he asked if he could come in here, to the room."

"He did?"

"Just wanted to clear it with you. I know Art is doing better, but I'm sure Dr. Halper wouldn't want any commotion. Sometimes family situations can—"

"I don't think Rick would do anything like that. You can let him in."

"Okay."

"Thanks, Holly." Leanne turned and walked toward the door. She wondered why Rick wanted to come in. He hated hospitals. And he hadn't come to Art's room since the day this whole ordeal began. She walked toward the doorway to meet him. She didn't want their conversation to awaken Art.

She looked back at him sleeping so contentedly. His belly full. Everything had stayed down, which Dr. Halper said would be a good sign.

"Mom?"

She turned to face Rick. Something seemed wrong. His eyes—he'd been crying. "Are you okay, Rick?"

He smiled. "I've brought your journal." He looked down at a bag in his left hand.

"Thanks, Rick. Holly said you want to come in. Art's asleep."

He took a few steps toward her. His smile disappeared. Tears filled his eyes. He dropped the bag. It made a thud as it hit the floor; there was something inside besides her journal. "Oh, Mom." He reached for her, put his arms around her, and began to cry. Then the cry became heaving sobs.

"Rick, what's wrong?" she said quietly. "What happened?"

"I'm so sorry," he said, his head buried in her shoulder.

She couldn't imagine what he'd done to make him this upset.

"For . . . " he said. "For all these years."

She patted his back gently. As she did, she realized they hadn't embraced this way for so long. The last time, she had been bending down to reach him, not reaching up. "It's okay, Rick," she said quietly. "Whatever it is. It'll be okay." Tears began to form in her eyes. Whatever this was, she could tell it was something big. She saw Holly over his shoulder, stepping around the counter, holding her hands up as if to say "Is everything all right?" Leanne nodded, reassuring her it was.

But she really wasn't sure. He just kept crying. She'd never seen him like this. Ever.

Finally, he lifted his head. Holly tiptoed over, holding out a handful of tissues. Leanne nodded her thanks, took them, and handed them to Rick.

"Mom, something happened tonight," he said, wiping his eyes and face. "I don't know where to begin." He took a step back. "Maybe I should start here." He bent down and pulled something out of the bag.

As soon as she saw it, her heart began to panic. The wooden box. He'd found it. She'd forgotten all about it. They had planned to talk to Rick about JD but wanted to give it more time, hoping they could get him some help. They didn't want him to find out this way. As he stood up, she realized . . . he wasn't angry with her. "Oh, Rick. I'm sorry. We meant to tell you about—"

"It's okay, Mom. We can talk about the details later. I'm not upset. I was at first, but I'm not anymore." Tears filled his eyes again. "I figured out what happened. What you and Art have done, are still trying to do with JD, with . . . my dad." He shook his head. "I've been a fool, a terrible son. To you . . . and especially to Art. For so long." He looked past her a moment, toward Art's bed.

Had he just said he'd been a terrible son . . . to Art? Leanne's heart began to fill with emotion. Hope and joy, a peaceful confusion. *Lord, what have you done to Rick?*

"And I've treated him so badly," he said, sighing heavily.

"Who?" she asked. It didn't seem he was referring to Art anymore.

"JD—my dad. I still have a hard time saying it. At the store. I didn't know who he was, and I . . . Andrea must hate me."

"She doesn't hate you, Rick."

"Has she told you how I've treated him? I've been calling him Columbo."

Leanne laughed out loud; she couldn't help it.

Rick laughed too. "It sounds funny now, but I did more than that. I chased him off, Mom."

"It's okay, Rick. It's been . . . complicated. For us too. Ever since he showed up last year."

"It's not okay."

"Well, Andrea doesn't hate you. She doesn't know who JD is, either. We didn't tell her very much about him. But . . ." Leanne paused. She didn't want to say too much about Andrea or say anything she might regret.

"Leanne?"

It was Art. She turned around. Apparently, they had started talking too loudly.

"Maybe I should go," Rick whispered, taking a step back. "I don't want to upset him or cause him any setbacks."

"Actually, he's doing a lot better. He's not near as fragile as he was before the surgery. I think he might like to see you . . . if you're up to it." She turned back toward Art. "Someone's here to see you, Art."

"Wait a minute," Rick said. "I forgot something in the waiting room." He put the wooden box back in the bag and handed it to her. Then rushed off toward the waiting room.

Leanne hurried over to Art's bed. "Art, you're not going to believe this. Something wonderful has happened to Rick. Are you okay? Do you feel okay?"

"Yeah, just a little tired, as usual. What's happened?"

"God's doing something," she said in an excited whisper, leaning over his bed. "He found the box, the one in his top dresser drawer."

"The one with JD's stuff in it?" His eyes instantly showed alarm.

"Yes, but it's okay. Really." She heard footsteps, turned to see Rick in the doorway. "Are you up to seeing him?"

"Sure," Art said. "I think so."

Leanne nodded for Rick to come in. She was surprised to see him empty-handed and wondered what he'd forgotten back in the waiting room. Rick walked toward the bed, slowly, almost apprehensively. His eyes filled with tears again as he drew near. She stepped back to give him some room.

This was an amazing moment. She'd prayed for Rick's heart to change for so many years, had given up on everything but prayer to bring about that change.

"Hi, Art," Rick said, a tear sliding down his cheek.

"Hi, Rick. Good to see you."

Rick looked as if he were thinking of something light to say back, but his emotions took over. His shoulders slumped. "I'm sorry, Art," he said through tears. He sat on the chair next to the bed, rested his hand on the edge. "I've been so wrong about you, for so many years."

Leanne looked at Art, and he looked back at her. He was smiling. Tears were in his eyes. He patted Rick's hand. "It's okay, Rick."

Rick looked up. "It's not okay. You didn't deserve what you got from me, the way I treated you. What I want to say now is . . . I just want to say I'm sorry." He stood up. "And I want to say thank you." He looked at his mom. "Thanks for all the years you've loved my mom. You've taken wonderful care of her."

Leanne started to cry.

"I saw all the photographs on the wall in the hallway. She looked so happy . . . in every one."

"She's very easy to love," Art said.

"And thanks for what you're trying to do for JD . . . my dad. I know what you've been trying to do down at the store."

"We planned to tell you about it," Art said. "It's just—"

"We can talk about it later, when you're better. The most important thing I want to say is . . . well, here, let me show you." He stepped back from the bed and walked toward the hallway. He reached for something out of view.

Leanne couldn't believe her eyes. She was about to lose it altogether. She looked over at Art; tears began to stream down his face when he saw what Rick held in his hand.

"You need to get better, Art, real soon," Rick said. He was holding two fishing poles. "You and I have a lot of catching up to do."

43

It was Friday morning. Rick was driving slowly through the downtown area. Sitting on the seat beside him, a white McDonald's bag with three Egg McMuffins. He'd hardly slept a wink last night. He was emotionally spent; he thought that would mean he'd sleep like a baby. Instead he tossed and turned for hours. In desperation, he'd even tried three rounds with the Magic Fingers. Of course, it didn't help. He'd been tempted to finish off a bottle of rum he'd bought last week, but that didn't feel right.

He kept thinking about JD. What his life had become, how it could have turned out that way, the horrible way Rick had treated him.

Before Rick had left the hospital, his mom and Art had given him a few more details about the situation. Art had done most of the talking. But really, there wasn't a whole lot to tell. It wasn't like they'd been able to have coherent conversations with JD, in which he could spell out how and why his life had spiraled out of control since he'd left Rick and Leanne all those years ago. He had just showed up at the store one day, pretty much in his present condition. A homeless guy looking for a handout.

On that day, Art had arrived at the store to open up. JD

had been sleeping in the stairwell. A brief conversation occurred. That's when Art first met his invisible friend, Taylor. He didn't know it at first. It was maybe a week or two before he figured out who Taylor was. Art continued to see JD for the next several mornings, but Leanne wasn't with him. Often, she didn't get to the store until a few hours later. By then JD would be gone. The next Saturday morning, she did come in with Art and was shocked when she realized who he'd been talking about.

Art had been trying to win JD's confidence ever since. So far, he'd only been able to convince him to let Art hold his "important papers" for safekeeping. JD had to think about it for a few days, said Taylor finally talked him into saying yes. Art had hopes of eventually getting JD to a doctor, to see if they could put him on some medication for his schizophrenia. Maybe get him out of that cardboard box to a halfway house.

A blaring horn snapped Rick out of his thoughts. As he drove through the intersection, he waved to the man in the car behind him, an apology for not seeing the light had turned green. Rick couldn't find his father anywhere. He looked at the bag of food sitting beside him. By now it had to be cold. He sighed as he turned the car around and headed back to the store to open up.

That first pot of coffee needed to be strong.

———— ▲ ————

"JD is *who*?"

"He's my father. Just saying it . . . I still can't believe it." Rick had thought he was getting used to the idea as the day wore on. Andrea's reaction reminded him of how weird this whole thing was.

Rick was glad the store was empty. He filled her in on everything he'd learned about JD so far. "Can you hand me that box of tissues?" he asked. "Think I'm going to need them for this next part." What was he saying? Rick never cried. Now he was asking for tissues in advance. He did his best to explain what happened on the pier by the river last night, then later at the hospital. He did all right, till the end. He completely lost it when he got to the part about the fishing poles.

And so did she. As Rick mopped up, he wondered what Andrea must think of him.

"Rick, that is so wonderful," she said, and threw her arms around him and cried some more.

Not the reaction he'd expected, but . . . he'd take it.

After a few minutes, she got control of herself and pulled back. Rick handed her a few more tissues. "Your parents must have been thrilled, especially Art."

"Seemed like they were," he said. Then an odd thought. He didn't feel the urge to correct her for referring to Art as his parent. "But I'm still struggling."

"About JD?"

He nodded. "I've got to find him. I've got to try to make things right."

She held up a small trash can. They tossed their tissues in it. "If you do, are you going to tell him he's your dad?"

"I don't know. I don't think so. I'm not sure how he'd take it. My mom's not even sure if he remembers who *she* is. She said he avoids her completely and will only come near Art. Right now, I just want to apologize, see if I can get him to start coming back."

"I'll help you."

"You will?"

"I'll call Amy's sitter and see if she can stay there for dinner. I know most of the places that feed the homeless around here. We can stop by each one. If he's not there, I'll tell them if they see JD to say Andrea said he can come back to the store tomorrow, that it's okay. He knows me. He might listen if they tell him I said it."

"Thanks, Andrea." He wanted to hug her again but didn't. "I'll pick up some fresh Egg McMuffins on the way in tomorrow." Rick looked at his watch. He decided it was time to do something he'd been avoiding all day.

"What's the matter?" she asked.

"I've got to call my boss."

"What for?"

Rick shook his head then sighed. "I know Art's doing better, but it looks like he's going to be in the hospital another few days, if not another week."

"You going to ask for more time off?"

"I'm going to try." The little bell above the door rang. An elderly woman walked in.

"I'll take care of her, you go make your call."

Rick decided to use the phone back in the office. He stared at the receiver a few moments, trying to think of what to say. Nothing came. He picked it up and dialed the number. Within a few seconds, the secretary put him through. He hoped Mr. Rainey might be in a TGIF mood.

"Hello, Jim Rainey here. How can I help you?"

"It's Rick, Mr. Rainey. Rick Denton."

"Rick," he said in a pleasant tone. "Where are you?"

"Still in Florida, sir."

"You wrapping things up?"

"Umm . . . it does look like my stepfather is going to make it after all."

"So, you'll be back here Monday?"

"If I need to be."

"What's that mean, Rick?" The pleasantness was gone.

"He's still in the hospital, Mr. Rainey. I was hoping to give my mother a few more days to be with him."

"Is he dying?"

"Doesn't look that way."

"Then I think you need a little help keeping track of your

priorities. See you back here on Monday." Then a click. He had hung up.

So much for TGIF, Rick thought. He got up and walked toward the front of the store.

Andrea had just finished with some customers at the counter. After they exited the store, she said, "Looks like it didn't go so well."

"It didn't. He pretty much ordered me back Monday."

"Would he fire you if you didn't come back?"

"Something like that."

"Don't worry about it, Rick. We'll make out somehow."

Rick appreciated what she said. But she had a look on her face that didn't quite line up with her words.

44

Rick turned left at the now familiar downtown intersection, saw the morning sun lighting up the church steeple ahead on the right. As he got closer, he saw Andrea's car parked next to the Book Nook. Last night had been wonderful and disappointing at the same time.

The disappointment was, they had spent two hours visiting every charity and street ministry in the area; no one had seen JD all day. The upside was spending two hours driving around with Andrea. Then afterward, she had agreed to grab a quick bite to eat with him before heading back to her babysitter to get Amy.

As they ate, Rick mentioned he was still planning to bring the Egg McMuffins in this morning. Andrea had suggested they get there thirty minutes early. If JD wasn't at the store, they could take a quick drive around to all the downtown charities that served breakfast. It shouldn't take long; it was less than half the number who served dinner.

Rick pulled in behind Andrea's car. As he got out, she was coming around the corner of the building, shaking her head. "Sorry, Rick. He's not here."

Rick sighed. Where could he be? "Hope he hasn't skipped town. If he has, I may never find him."

She looked at her watch. "You ready to take that drive?" Rick nodded. "Let me get in there and make a quick note," she said, looking toward the front door.

"What for?"

"In case we're a little late getting back. Not many customers come in this early on Saturday, but in case any do."

"Good idea." He watched her head down the steps and unlock the door. It was the strangest thing, and the strangest time for something like this to dawn on him. But as he watched her walk into the store, he realized, very clearly . . . he was in love with her. That was what these feelings were. He'd been attracted to dozens of women over the years, even felt strong feelings for a few of them.

But nothing had ever come close to this.

The clarity in his heart just then was strong enough that if he'd heard a minister ask, "Will you forsake all others and cling only to her for as long as you both shall live?" Rick felt he could immediately and with certainty say, "I will."

She came out of the store and looked up at him. "What?" she said.

"What?" he said back.

"You're smiling now," she said. "You looked so upset before." She turned and relocked the door.

"Just had a funny thought," he said.

"Care to tell me?" She climbed the steps. "Think I could use a smile about now."

I would love to tell you, he thought, but he knew if he did, she'd run for the hills. "It's nothing. Want to take my car?"

"Of course," she said, giving her car a disparaging look.

They got in. Andrea set the McDonald's bag on her lap and Rick drove off. "Got an extra one in there for you, if you want it."

"I'm starving. Sure you don't mind?"

"Not at all. Ate mine on the way."

"There's three of them in here."

"One for you, one for JD, and an extra one for Taylor."

"That was sweet, Rick."

Rick pulled out onto the road. "I hope we find him. You're going to have to tell me where to stop."

It took about twenty-five minutes to make all their stops. Once again, no luck. And the worst part, no one had seen JD for the last few days.

"Where could he be?" Andrea said as they headed back to the store.

"Maybe I scared him off for good," said Rick. "Maybe he decided to call it quits and head south."

"Maybe, but didn't you tell him he could start coming back when Art got better?"

"Yeah . . . while I was yelling at him to get lost." He wished he'd known then what he knew now. Or better yet, that he hadn't been such a jerk in the first place.

"Say, Rick, something just popped into my head. Remember when the store got robbed and you went out looking for JD? Didn't you find him in the park, the one near the river?"

"Yes." Rick quickly pulled into the right-hand lane and turned at the next intersection. "Certainly worth a try."

It wasn't far, less than a mile. He pulled into the same parking area as before, but there weren't any other cars. They got out, and Rick looked around. He didn't see anyone.

"Want me to bring this?" Andrea asked, holding the bag of food.

"I don't know. Might as well, but it doesn't look too promising."

He walked first to the area where he'd spotted JD before: the cement wall that ran along the river. Then over by the playground, then by the fountain. No luck.

"I don't know, Andrea," he said, sighing heavily. "Think this is a lost cause."

"Wait a minute," she said. She put her hands on either side of her mouth and yelled. "JD! Are you here?"

Wow, could she make some noise.

"JD!" she yelled again. "It's Andrea . . . from the Book Nook. Are you here? I want to talk to you!"

Rick turned around. Behind him, deep within a thick cluster of trees and scrub palms, he heard a crackling sound.

Andrea heard it too. "JD . . . is that you? It's Andrea."

"Taylor, you hear that?"

"I did. You're being summoned."

"What's that even mean?"

The voice called out again. "JD . . . is that you? It's Andrea."

"It's Andrea," JD said. "From the bookstore. What day is it?"

"It's Saturday," Taylor said. "I think we overslept. I told you we might if we stayed here. The sun can't even get through all these trees. I'll bet we missed breakfast."

"But it's Andrea, from the Book Nook. That's right, she works on Saturdays. She's almost as nice as Art. But what's she doing here, in this place?"

"JD," she called again. "Got something for you."

"Why don't you go find out?" Taylor said.

JD took a few steps toward her voice. "You coming?" he said, turning to Taylor.

"I don't recall hearing my name. Go see what she wants. Like you said, she's a nice person. When a nice person calls your name, saying they have something for you, it's usually something nice."

JD took a few more steps, wrapped his blanket a little

tighter around his shoulders. "Andrea?" he yelled back. "I'm in here, in these woods."

"I'm guessing you haven't had breakfast yet," she said. "Brought you some."

Okay, JD thought, Taylor was right. "I'm coming." He carefully stepped through the wet leaves and broken branches, pushed aside the palm fronds, tried to keep them from slapping him in the face. Finally, he got through it all.

"Hi, JD," Andrea said, smiling. "Here." She held up a familiar white bag.

Wait a minute, JD thought. She wasn't alone. He rubbed his eyes and looked again. "Aahh!" he screamed and ran back into the woods. He tripped over a big root, fell flat on his face. It was that young man who'd been working at the store, the one who hated him. Taylor was wrong. She wasn't nice, she'd tricked him.

"Wait, JD, it's okay," she yelled. "Please come back, Rick is sorry!"

JD pushed himself up but slipped again, his feet all tripped up in the blanket.

"JD, it's me, Rick. Please come back. Please!" the guy shouted. "I was wrong to treat you the way I did. I wanna make it up to you. Please come back."

JD stopped and thought a moment. If he wasn't mistaken, the guy sounded sincere. Maybe it wasn't a trick.

"Rick really is sorry, JD," Andrea said. "If you trust me at all, please come back. I would never do anything to hurt you."

"Please, JD . . . Please," said the man with her.

It was that Rick fellow. He sounded different, nicer. JD got up and turned around. "Okay, then, I'll come out." He rewrapped his blanket around him, then made his way back to the wood's edge. Andrea was standing there holding the McDonald's bag in one hand. The other was wrapped around the shoulder of the young man, Rick.

"I'm here," he said.

Rick looked up. He wiped his eyes on his jacket sleeve. There was his father, looking just as bad as he ever did, maybe worse. But all Rick felt in his heart was compassion now. That and sadness. But he set the sadness aside. He had to get control of himself, didn't want to scare him off again. He walked slowly toward JD.

"Here, Rick." Andrea handed him the white bag.

Rick held it out as JD got closer. "Egg McMuffins, JD. Just the way you like 'em. And hash browns too."

"Hash browns?" JD said, a smile now appearing.

"And there's an extra one in there for Taylor."

JD took the bag. He stunk something awful.

"For Taylor too?"

Dad . . . Rick thought, looking into JD's eyes. Don't you know who I am? He wanted so bad to tell him, to understand what had happened to him. But he forced these thoughts away. Now was not the time.

"Thank you," JD said, then turned back toward the woods.

"Before you go," Rick said, "I want to tell you something. If you don't mind, I'd like to tell you with you looking right at me."

JD turned around, a nervous look on his face. He looked at Rick, then away. Rick waited a few moments, didn't say anything. JD looked at him again.

"I am so sorry for how I treated you, JD. From the first moment we met till now. You are someone Art cares about a lot, and that should have been enough for me. It's not your fault that it wasn't. It's mine. You can come back to the store."

"I can?"

"Today, in fact."

"I'd sure like to be back there," he said. "Way more than these woods."

"Well, you come back then. You're Art's honored guest. That's how you'll be treated from now on by everyone at the Book Nook, including me."

"Art gonna be okay?"

"Looks that way. He's healing up pretty good. From what I've heard, you're the one who saved his life."

"Me?"

"That's what I heard. So you come back to us, okay?"

JD looked down at the ground. "Okay then."

"When you get all set up, you come knock on the door at the store. I'll come out with a fresh cup of coffee."

"Well, okay then." JD held out his hand. His dirty, grimy hand.

Rick felt like he was about to lose it completely. He choked back the tears, reached out, and shook it. *God*, he prayed silently as JD headed back for the woods, *please show us how to help him. There's got to be something we can do.*

45

"It's all finished, Mr. Rick. Wanna see it?"

Rick smiled, looking down at Amy sitting on the sofa, her homemade Christmas catalog spread out on the coffee table. Andrea had to pick her up at lunch; the babysitter had a Christmas party to attend that afternoon, somewhere out of town. "Don't you think you better cover Annabelle's eyes first?" he said, pointing to her doll. "She's looking right at it."

Amy quickly closed the catalog, then shoved a pillow over Annabelle's face. Rick laughed. Good thing Annabelle didn't need to breathe.

"Okay, now come look at it."

Rick pushed the start button on the coffeemaker and sat next to Amy. "All right, let's see what you got here." He picked up the catalog and started slowly turning the pages. Amy scooted closer to him, pointing at each toy on the page, filling him in on the most important details. She had a lot to say, and Rick realized he enjoyed hearing every bit.

He didn't know if he and Amy's mom had any chance of a future together, but he realized just then that he desperately hoped they might. He'd love to be involved in this little girl's life somehow. The fear of what that meant had vanished. But it wasn't because of anything he had done. It was Amy.

Her attitude toward him had been so kind and accepting, so completely the opposite from how he'd treated Art when he'd first come into Rick's life.

"So what do you think?" she said, looking up at him with her beautiful bright blue eyes.

"I think someday Mr. J.C. Penney should hire you to do catalogs for him."

"Really?"

"It's very good, Amy. How old are you again?"

"Six."

"It's way too good for a six-year-old. You've got to be at least eleven or twelve."

"No, silly, I'm just six."

"Okay, if you say so. But you know what?"

"What?"

"I didn't see any check marks or stars next to any of the toys. How do you know which ones Annabelle wants most for Christmas?"

"Oh, I know."

"Are you sure?"

"Sure I'm sure. I know Annabelle really good."

"Still . . . you don't wanna forget something that important. I think you should take a few minutes and mark the ones you know she really wants."

"What should I write?"

"Know how to make stars?" Amy nodded. "Well, put one star by the one she wants the most, two stars for the second best one, three stars for the third . . . like that."

"Okay, I'll do it right now."

"I'm going to go up front, see if your mom needs any help."

"I'm right here," Andrea said.

Rick looked up. She was standing in the middle of the main aisle, smiling. Then she got a concerned look on her face. "I just realized, today is your last day here, isn't it?"

"It is?" Amy said loudly.

"Yes, it is," Rick said.

"It can't be," Amy said. "Why is it your last day?"

"I have to go back to my old job on Monday."

"Where's that?"

"In Charlotte, where I live."

"You don't live here?"

"No, I don't."

"Where's Charlotte? Is it far?"

"In another state."

"Aren't you going to be here for Christmas?" she asked.

Rick looked up at Andrea. Her face looked genuinely sad. She was sad he was leaving. "I'm gonna come back," he said, "and spend Christmas here."

"You are?" Amy and Andrea said in unison.

"That's the plan. But if I don't go back and finish my work in Charlotte, I'll lose my job."

"Can't you just make this your new job?" said Amy.

"He can't, Amy," Andrea said. "Rick has a really important job. And Art's getting better, so pretty soon, he'll be back here at the store."

Rick stood up.

"But you promise you're coming back for Christmas, right?" Amy asked.

Promise? Rick thought. Could he promise something like that?

"Say you promise," Amy repeated.

Rick looked at Andrea, then back at Amy's pleading little face. "Okay, I promise."

He looked at Andrea again, but she had turned around and headed back toward the front of the store.

46

Rick stepped out of the elevator at the hospital. As he waited for the nurse to buzz him through to the ICU, he was aware of another change he felt inside. He wasn't hating being in a hospital as much. He felt a little tense, but that was all. He walked around the corner. The nurse at the counter smiled as he came to Art's doorway. "Is it okay?" he whispered.

"You can go in."

He saw his mom in the far corner, reading a book. A curtain pulled out from the wall blocked most of Art's bed. Rick stepped up quietly.

As soon as she noticed him, his mom got a big smile. "Rick," she said and stood up.

He stepped closer, and they hugged. He glanced at Art still asleep.

"What have you got there?" his mom asked.

"The latest issue of *Field & Stream*. I didn't see any magazines here the last time I came."

"That was sweet of you." She was talking at a normal volume.

"Aren't you concerned he'll wake up?" he said quietly.

"No, he's been sleeping all day. He still needs rest, but the doctor said I don't have to tiptoe around anymore. We got some good news this afternoon."

"What is it?"

"They're moving him out of the ICU tomorrow morning. He goes to a regular bed on the second floor."

"Really?" Rick said. "That's some serious progress."

"Isn't it wonderful?"

"Have they noticed any other problems, because of the surgery?"

"He still can't taste his food, the poor dear. But the doctor did some checking, and sometimes things like that come back later on." She walked over to Art's bedside. "Hey, Art," she said, patting him on the arm. "Look who's here, hon. It's Rick."

His eyes fluttered then opened. He focused on her face and smiled. "Did I fall asleep again?"

"A few hours ago. Are you up for a little visit?"

He awoke more fully then turned and looked at Rick.

"Hi, Art," Rick said. "How ya feeling?"

"Not too bad, Rick." He sat up a little. "Food's lousy here, all tastes the same, but other than that, I'm doing okay for an almost-dead guy."

"Stop, Art," his mom said. "Look what Rick brought you." She handed him the magazine.

A big smile. "This the new issue?"

"Think so," said Rick.

"Say," Art said, turning to Leanne. "Am I even allowed to read yet?"

"You know, I'm not sure. You better just look at the pictures till we ask Dr. Halper."

He started flipping the pages.

"Not now, Art. We've got company."

"Well, I can't stay but a few minutes," Rick said. "Really came to say good-bye."

"Do you have to go already?" his mom said.

"Got to be back 8:00 Monday morning. Gotta pack and hit the road first thing tomorrow."

"Well, don't you worry about us, Rick," Art said. "You heard they're moving me to a regular room tomorrow?"

"I did."

"I've already talked with Andrea," his mom said. "I'm going to come in to see Art every morning. We'll open the store at 10:00 instead of 9:00, give me a little more time here. She's going to ask her boss at the diner if he'll let her out every day at 2:00 p.m. sharp. We'll manage till Art is out of bed. Don't you worry."

"I really wish I could have stayed longer, but my boss made the decision for me. It was either come back Monday or don't come back at all. But, I am planning on coming for Christmas. That's only nine or ten days away. If it's all right, that is."

"All right?" Art said. "That would be wonderful."

"Rick . . . " His mom had tears in her eyes. "That'll make this the best Christmas we've had in years. You coming home and—"

"Me not being dead," Art said.

"And you not being dead," his mom said.

"I'm looking forward to it."

"But this time, when you come back, would you do your mother a big favor? It can be my Christmas present."

"What is it?"

"Would you stay with us, instead of at a hotel?"

"It will be a sacrifice, but I think I can manage." They didn't see he was joking. "I mean, I'd have to give up the Magic Fingers."

They laughed. "I forgot all about that thing," his mother said. "You and your father used to love doing that. I didn't know they still had those."

"Only at the finest motels," Rick said. "Well, I've gotta

go." He walked over and gave his mom a big hug. She started crying softly. "It's okay, Mom. I'll be back soon."

"It's not that. I'm just so grateful . . . for everything you've done. I would have never made it through all this without you."

"I'm glad I could help." He walked over to Art.

"Rick . . . there aren't words . . . " His eyes filled with tears too.

"Now, let's don't do this," he said, choking back his own. He reached out his hand. Art took it and pulled him closer.

"Thank you," Art said. "For everything."

Rick walked out into the hall, thinking, Can't believe he's thanking me.

━━━━━━━▲━━━━━━━

About an hour later, Art was asleep again. Leanne was reading her book. Art had finished his obligatory dinner a little while ago. Still couldn't taste it. Leanne had assured him, considering what they had served tonight, it was a blessing. She was definitely looking forward to cooking her own food again at home.

She looked up, surprised to see Andrea standing in the doorway, a concerned expression on her face. Andrea motioned for Leanne to come to her, obviously not wanting to talk in front of Art. "Is everything okay, dear?" Leanne asked.

"I can't stay. I've got Amy in the waiting room."

"You seem . . . a little upset."

"I'm not really. Concerned, maybe . . . confused."

"What's the matter?"

Andrea looked around, as if they were talking too loud. "Rick is leaving tomorrow."

"I know." Leanne had forgotten; Andrea had begun to have feelings for him. "Does that worry you?" She spoke softly.

Andrea nodded.

"Are you afraid that going back to Charlotte will be too much for him? That he'll get sucked back into . . . his old world?"

Andrea nodded her head. "It's like we don't even have to talk," she said. "Can you just read my mind? Is that it?" She was smiling again.

"I've been struggling a bit about the same thing."

"It's just so soon," Andrea said. "The change in him the last two days has been so wonderful, but what'll happen when he starts getting around all his old friends, all that money and power, the greed, all the . . ."

"Women?"

"He is a handsome man," Andrea said. "Put it together with everything else . . ."

"There is a lot to worry about," Leanne said.

"I wouldn't be as concerned if he had been here for a month or two after his change of heart, even a week or two. But two days? It doesn't seem long enough. Like pouring cement and then building the house before it hardens." She stopped and looked over her shoulder. "Hold on a minute, let me go check on Amy."

Leanne watched her walk back toward the waiting room. Andrea leaned into the waiting room doorway. When she pulled back out, she was smiling. "She's fine," Andrea said as she returned.

"Andrea, I understand your concerns. I've thought the same things, but really, it's out of our hands."

"I know, I know." She looked away. "I just wish it wasn't so soon."

"All we can really do is pray," said Leanne.

"I know," Andrea said.

But she said it as though she didn't believe it could possibly be enough.

Andrea walked back to the waiting room to get Amy. She stood in the doorway, looking down at Amy's face as she looked up, responding to Andrea calling her name. Amy was so happy, so trusting, eyes so full of hope. Had Andrea ever looked at life that way?

"What's wrong, Mom?"

"Nothing, sweetheart, it's just time to go."

"Is Mr. Art okay?"

"He's doing much better."

"God's answering all of our prayers, isn't he?" Amy said.

"He is," Andrea said. As they walked to the elevator, it dawned on her. God really had been answering their prayers . . . about Art. But she hadn't prayed about Rick, hardly at all. All she'd done was worry. And be afraid about her future.

Once again, here she was, Much Afraid, tormented and harassed by the Fearings all around her. Just like the character in Hannah Hurnard's book. She'd even been afraid to pray about Rick, afraid of the feelings she was having for him, afraid of where her heart might go if she let it run free. She pushed the elevator button.

She was tired of being Much Afraid. If she couldn't trust the Chief Shepherd with her heart, at least enough to start praying about her fears, then who could she trust?

47

6 Days Later

Leanne looked at Art resting comfortably at home in his favorite rocking chair, next to the fireplace. Yesterday, Dr. Halper had released him from the hospital, confident he was strong enough to convalesce here. When they walked through the front door yesterday, she was overcome with emotion, almost as excited as the day she had first moved in with Rick, right after the wedding. Such a comfortable and comforting place, so many good memories. She was so grateful God had given them a fresh opportunity to make some new ones together. And only three days before Christmas.

She walked back to the kitchen, picked up Art's favorite mug, and filled it to the brim, then walked out and set it beside him. Johnny Mathis serenaded them on the hi-fi. He had just sung "*The weather outside is frightful.*" But it wasn't. She looked out the window and smiled. Sunny, in the high sixties.

Art looked up from his magazine. "Oh my goodness," he said. "I have longed for this moment." He set the magazine on his lap and reached for the mug. He held it under his nose and inhaled deeply. "Leanne . . . this smell is more sweet to me than your most expensive perfume." He took a sip. "I can't even believe how good this tastes . . . Hey!" he shouted, almost spilling his coffee. "I can taste it, Leanne! I can really taste it."

"You can?"

He took another sip. "Yes," he said again loudly. Then another sip. "Oh thank you, Lord!" Then another sip.

Leanne smiled. "An early Christmas gift," she said.

"Aren't you forgetting something?" he asked.

"I don't think so."

"You've been torturing me out here for the last twenty minutes with the smell of those orange sweet rolls."

"You can have some when Andrea and Amy come over to decorate the tree."

"I feel bad you having to wrap those lights around the tree yourself. That's my job."

"Well, next year you can have it back. I'm just glad you're here to watch." Art also had to let go of another tradition this year—putting up the decorations outside. He would trim the whole front of the house in lights, even used to lace them throughout the trees. Something of a friendly competition going on with the neighbors on either side. Leanne wouldn't mind if he gave up this tradition altogether. She hated him getting up on that ladder.

"Heard anything from Rick?" he asked.

"No," Leanne said, walking back toward the kitchen. She picked up her mug, came back, and sat on the part of the sofa closest to Art's chair. "Andrea asked me the same thing when I invited her over this afternoon. Haven't heard a word since he went back to Charlotte."

"Rick was never one to talk much on the phone," Art said.

"I know, but . . ."

"I'm sure he's all right, hon."

"I want to believe that," said Leanne. "It really did seem like something big had happened with him last week." She thought about calling him herself but was afraid of what she might find.

"Something big *did* happen," Art said.

"He was the Rick I've been praying to see all these years."

"Leanne, don't worry. Just because he hasn't called doesn't mean anything. He's probably just been really busy. He took off two whole weeks to come down here in one of the busiest times of year for his line of work. He's probably just getting caught up."

"That's almost exactly what I told Andrea this afternoon."

"Now you don't believe it?"

"I wasn't that sure when I said it to her." She took a sip of coffee. "You know she's having feelings for him, don't you?"

"Kind of figured that one out," he said. "You afraid of her getting hurt, I guess."

"Well, he's been gone for over ten years, Art. Got his whole life set just the way he always wanted it up there. We only talk on the phone a few times a year, and even then, I could always tell he couldn't wait to hang up. You should have seen him when he first got here. He was . . . so hard. Like someone I hardly knew."

"But that's not the Rick I saw in the hospital last week," Art said.

"I know," she said. But still she worried. Like Andrea, Leanne wished he didn't have to go back to it all so soon.

48

Christmas Eve

Another beautiful day. Sunny but with a nice chill in the air. Just what you want at Christmas. That was the thing living in Florida. Forget about snow. More than half the Christmases were so warm, you didn't even need a sweater. Tourists from up north loved it. Sometimes they'd even swim in the ocean on Christmas Day. It made for a lovely postcard to send to friends up north, but, having grown up in Ohio, Leanne preferred the weather a little chilly at Christmas.

At the moment, she was finishing up the dishes. Andrea had insisted she be allowed to help, but Leanne pulled rank. "You go on, watch that Rudolph show with Amy and Art." It was that stop-motion version that came on CBS every year, the one with Burl Ives as a singing snowman and that little elf who wanted to be a dentist. It had been Rick's favorite Christmas show when he was young.

Leanne sighed.

Still no word from Rick. Eight days now.

They barely talked about it at the dinner table. No one wanted to upset Amy. She was completely convinced Rick was still coming tomorrow. "He promised me," she'd said, the one time it came up. Like that settled it. Leanne had invited Andrea and Amy to spend Christmas Eve with them, so Amy could wake up to a nicer Christmas morning. Andrea's apartment was so small and she didn't have money to decorate it well. During dinner, Art had asked how long they were staying. Amy jumped right in with the answer: "We can only stay tonight, right, Mommy? Mr. Rick is coming here tomorrow for Christmas, so he'll need his old room back, right?"

Andrea and Leanne immediately looked at each other, uncertain about what to say. "That's right," Art had said reassuringly.

Perhaps Amy had sensed their apprehension. "Mr. Rick *is* coming tomorrow, Mommy. He promised me."

Children and their childlike faith, Leanne thought. She dried the last dish and set it on the rack beside the sink. Over the last several days, her own faith had waned to where she felt now it was the better part of wisdom to give up on Rick showing up altogether. She'd reduced her hopes to the dutiful phone call she'd get, like she did every year, prepared herself for the excuses he'd offer about why he couldn't come home after all.

She poured herself a cup of decaf coffee and walked through the dining room to join the others. She loved how the living room looked through the doorway. Art sat in his overstuffed armchair, legs propped up on the ottoman, watching Rudolph, laughing out loud at the slightest joke. Amy sat on the oval throw rug, her back resting against the ottoman. Andrea was on the sofa, looking up at the show every now and then over some embroidered gift she was making.

The house was finally decorated just the way she liked it. At the far left corner of the room stood the fireplace. Beside it, the tree looked wonderful, even without the lights wrapped around the top eighteen inches. She knew it bugged Art that she wouldn't let him get up on the ladder to finish it, but he didn't complain. And there in front of the fireplace, Art's wooden rocker sat awaiting a roaring fire. He insisted they light one tomorrow, even if they had to turn the air conditioning on for a few hours to make it cold enough.

Everything looked perfect. Except . . . Rick.

"Aren't you coming in, hon?" Art asked.

"Sure," she said. "Just enjoying the scenery."

"Dinner was wonderful," Andrea said.

"Especially the mashed potatoes," Amy said.

"Why, thank you." Leanne sat on the other end of the sofa. "Wait till you taste my lasagna tomorrow."

"What is that?" Amy said.

"It's a fancy Italian dish I make every Christmas Day. You like spaghetti and meat sauce?"

Amy nodded.

"Then you're going to love my lasagna."

Amy's attention was lured back to the television. "Look, Mom!" Amy shouted. "Barbie's Dream House." Her eyes lit up.

"I see it," Andrea said, looking up, then quickly back down at her project.

Leanne felt bad. Andrea had talked to her about this. The dollhouse sold for one hundred dollars, hopelessly outpriced for Andrea's budget. Leanne and Art had discussed getting it for her . . . for about two seconds. With all their hospital bills, there was just no way.

"Look, Mom, Barbie's Super Vette. See it?"

Andrea did look up this time. "That's really nice, Amy." She looked at Leanne and smiled.

Leanne winked and smiled back. That was the car she and Art had bought for Amy, under twenty dollars.

"What are they doing showing toy commercials on Christmas Eve?" Art said. "Not like any stores would be open now."

"You'd be surprised," Andrea said. "Quite a few of the major department stores announced they'd be staying open till 9:00 tonight."

"That's terrible," Art said. "Christmas Eve. Folks should be off on Christmas Eve, spend it with their families."

"I agree," Andrea said.

Spend it with their families, Leanne thought. She was glad to have Andrea and Amy here tonight. They were almost like family now.

But she really missed Rick.

The phone rang.

Andrea instantly looked at Leanne. So did Art. "Want me to get it?" Art said.

It rang again.

"You stay there. I'll get it," Leanne said. *Please let it be Rick.* She picked up the receiver. "Hello?"

"Mom?"

"Rick!" She turned around. Everyone, even Amy, looked up at her.

"Sorry I haven't called you sooner. Things have been insane up here lately."

"Art said he thought you'd be really busy."

"How's Art doing, everything okay?"

"He's sitting right here, in his favorite chair."

"He's home? Art's home?"

"Yep. Been home for three days now."

"I'm so glad."

"So how's it looking . . . for you?"

Rick sighed. She heard it clearly. She braced herself.

"I really wished I could have gotten down there today to spend Christmas Eve with you guys, then be there in the morning."

"I understand, Rick. It's a real busy time for you."

"You have no idea," he said. "So many things to take care

of these past few days. But, I've only got a few more things to take care of tonight. Then I'm done."

"Does that mean . . . you're still coming?"

"Of course, I am," he said. "Nothing could stop me."

"He's coming!" Leanne shouted to everyone in the living room. Art smiled. Andrea's eyes started tearing up.

"Of course he is," Amy said. "He promised."

"Is that Amy?" Rick said. "Is she there?"

"Yes. She and Andrea are staying overnight."

"That's great," Rick said. "But . . . I really wish I could be there in the morning now. I didn't know they'd be there."

"Well, you just come when you can. Maybe give me a call when you're two or three hours out, and I'll start making the lasagna."

"You're making lasagna?"

"It's Christmas," Leanne said.

"Yes, it is," Rick said. "Well, I better go if I'm going to stay on track. I can't wait to see you all."

"Rick, I'm so happy you're coming." She couldn't help it. She started to cry.

"I don't think you could possibly be happier than I feel right now," Rick said. "Tell everyone I'll see them tomorrow, and tell them . . . I've got a huge surprise."

49

Leanne felt wonderfully rested.

She'd fallen asleep thanking God for Rick's call, woke up so grateful he was coming home today. But now she had work to do. It was Christmas morning. Art always did Christmas morning, and it had to be done just so. He wanted to do it badly, but she insisted he stay in bed. Doctor's orders. He could come out when it was all set up.

"You got the checklist, hon?" he asked as she put on her bathrobe.

He'd actually written a list. "Got it right here," she said. "Now you wait till I come back for you."

"I've been getting out of bed myself the last few days."

"Well, don't come out till I come back." She opened the door to the hallway.

"Merry Christmas, my love," he said.

She walked back to the bed, leaned over, and gave him a hug. "Merry Christmas, Art. So glad you're here." After the hug, she said, "Now you stay put." She stepped into the hall, heard Rick's bedroom door open slightly. She heard giggles.

"Can I come out now?" It was little Amy.

"Not yet, sweetheart."

"How long?"

"Your mommy awake yet?"

"Barely." She heard Andrea's voice through the door.

"You've got a few minutes, Andrea. Art wants me to set things up."

"A few minutes?" Amy said. "Then can I come out?"

"Yes, but wait till I come get you."

"Close the door, Amy," Andrea said. "No peeking."

"All right." The door closed.

Leanne walked into the living room. Morning light had already begun to slip through the sheers, casting a soft glow on every object in the room. Such wonderfully familiar things. She and Art had bought all of them together. She'd rearranged them a half-dozen times before she'd gotten it just right.

She loved this room. Especially today.

It was chilly enough that they didn't have to turn on the air conditioning. Art had wanted a little nip in the house so they could use the fireplace. Felt like more than a little nip to her. She tightened her robe then turned on the lamp next to Art's chair, illuminating the mahogany end table. The home for Art's coffee mug. But today, it would transform into an almost sacred place.

It was the throne for the eggnog.

She smiled as she walked out to the kitchen to start the coffee. Art and his eggnog. He loved it so much, he thought everyone else must too. Years ago, he'd purchased a fancy crystal pitcher with four matching goblets. Unlike most years, this morning she'd get to pour the precious elixir into all four.

"Can we come out yet?" Amy yelled from the hall.

"Not yet, sweetie."

As the smell of fresh coffee filled the kitchen, she brought the eggnog out to the table, poured then arranged everything just so, including the nutmeg. The real thing, not the powdered stuff. A little nut about the size of an acorn. Had its own special grater, with the word *Meg* etched in the metal.

She bent down and started the fire. This was her least favorite thing on his checklist. She loved the warmth and the look, but what a messy job.

"Now?" Amy pleaded.

"We're so close," she yelled back.

Once the fire seemed to burn on its own, she walked around the back of the Christmas tree and plugged it in. She backed up toward the hallway and took in the scene, including the smattering of presents under the tree.

Now they were ready. She turned toward the bedrooms. "Andrea, you ready?"

"I am."

"Art, you ready?"

"I don't hear any music."

"Oops."

"I don't need music," Amy said.

"I'm afraid Art does. Just be a sec." She hurried over and turned on the hi-fi. A few scratchy sounds then Perry Como started singing "There's No Place Like Home for the Holidays." She walked into the hallway and got Art's attention. He shuffled out of the bedroom and sat down in his chair.

"Okay! We're ready!"

Amy burst out of the bedroom door, screaming with glee. Ran right past Leanne, almost spinning her like a top. Andrea came out slowly, looking remarkably well for someone who had just woken up.

"Merry Christmas," she said and gave Leanne a hug.

"You too, dear," said Leanne.

"Is that coffee I smell?"

"Should be ready. You know where the mugs are."

"Got eggnog here too," Art said. "With real nutmeg."

"I'd love some," Andrea said. "After coffee."

Art stood up.

"Merry Christmas," Leanne said, reaching out her arms

to give him a hug. They walked together and stood arm-in-arm beside Andrea. All three watched Amy tearing into her small pile of presents.

"Don't open the biggest one," Andrea said. "That's from Art and Leanne. Give Art a chance to get his coffee and sit down. Then bring the present over to his chair."

"Okay, Mommy." Amy lifted it up. "It's so heavy." It was just a bit bigger than a large shoe box. "What is it?"

"Tell you what," Art said. "Bring it over here, Amy." He pushed his ottoman to the side. "I'll just sip on this delicious eggnog here, have my coffee in a few minutes." He sat back in his chair.

Amy carried the gift over and set it by Art's feet. Leanne looked back at the small pile of presents she'd already opened, the few things Andrea could afford. Some doll dresses for Annabelle. A pair of shiny white dress shoes for church. A hairbrush and a comb. A little make-believe makeup kit. She was glad she and Art had bought the Barbie car. Kids should have at least one big surprise gift at Christmas.

Andrea leaned over and whispered in Leanne's ear, "Look at her. Thank you so much."

"Glad to do it," Leanne whispered back.

"Now?" Amy said.

"Okay," said Andrea.

Amy ripped through the paper and screamed, "My Barbie Super Vette!" as soon as she saw the picture on the box. "Thank you, thank you, thank you," she said before she even finished unwrapping it. She stood up, gave Art the biggest hug. Then ran over and did the same with Leanne.

"You're welcome," Art said. "Aren't you going to finish opening it?"

Amy ran back and pulled it free from the paper.

Leanne went into the kitchen to wash her hands and get her own cup of coffee. "Want me to fix yours, Art?"

"No . . . still working on my eggnog. *So* glad I can taste it. Thank you, Lord."

Amy rolled her little Barbie Corvette across the throw rug toward her other presents. "Mom, look how many presents I got this year. I think it's the most I ever got."

"Are you happy?" Andrea asked.

"Uh-huh. Wish I knew I was getting this," she said, rolling the car back and forth. "Would have brought my Barbie and Ken over."

As Leanne stepped back into the living room, she thought she heard a car pull up in front of the house.

"You hear that?" Art said.

Leanne walked past him to one of the front windows and pulled the sheers back. "Rick!" she shouted. "It's Rick."

"Well, I'll be," Art said, slowly getting out of his chair. "He must have driven through the night."

Andrea rushed to the window on the other side of the door. "Is that a . . . he's got a U-Haul trailer hooked up to his car."

"Wonder what he's got inside," Art said.

"Guess that's the surprise," said Amy as she came up beside her mom and peered out the window.

50

Rick got out of the car and was met on the front porch by big hugs all around, except for Andrea, who offered a side hug. Rick felt like there was some affection in it. There was certainly something different in her eyes from when he'd seen her last.

"So what's all this?" Art said, pointing at the trailer.

"It's my surprise, but first . . . did I miss you guys exchanging gifts?"

"Just Amy," Andrea said.

"Perfect," Rick said. "Drove all night trying to get here in time."

"You must be exhausted," his mom said. "Want some coffee? Something to eat?"

"In a little bit." He walked over to Amy and bent down. "I need you to do something for me, young lady."

"Can we do it in the house?" his mom said. "Little chilly to be talking out here on the porch."

"Sure," Rick said. "But when we go in, Amy, I need you to hide your eyes." He stood up. "How about you go in my old room for a few minutes."

"That's where we slept last night," she said.

"Really? Well, can you go back in there a few more minutes?"

"What for?"

"You'll see."

"Is this part of your surprise?" Mom asked.

"It's Amy's part."

They walked inside; Amy ran into Rick's room and closed the door. "Mom, I've got some things to bring in from outside, some presents for Amy. When you hear me kick the door gently, can you open it? I'm going to have my hands full." He closed the door and ran back to the car. He was loving this. He opened the back door, carefully pulled out Barbie's Dream House, and walked it slowly back to the porch. It wasn't that heavy, but it was big and bulky. He almost lost his footing on the porch steps. He gently kicked the bottom of the front door.

"Rick, what is it?" his mother asked when she opened the door.

"I know what it is," Andrea said. "I can't believe . . . I can't believe you did this."

Rick couldn't see her face; it was blocked by the dollhouse. He couldn't tell if she was happy or upset. "Where's a good place to set it down?"

"Over here," said Art. He led Rick to the far side of the Christmas tree.

He stood up and looked at Andrea. She was crying. *Okay . . . what kind of tears are—*

She ran across the rug and wrapped her arms around him and cried some more. "I can't believe you did this. She's going to be so happy."

He was really loving this now.

"It's beautiful, Rick," his mom said.

"Can I come out now?"

"Not yet," Rick said.

Andrea pulled back. Mom handed her a tissue.

"There's more," Rick said and ran out the front door. He brought back two large JCPenney bags and a big box. "I didn't have time to wrap any of this."

"What is it?" Andrea asked as he carried them through the door.

Rick started pulling the rest of the toys out of the bags. "Can you set these up around the tree, make it look nice?" he asked Andrea. "They're things from Amy's handmade catalog . . . for Annabelle. She showed it to me that last day in the store. I asked her to put stars by all the things Annabelle wanted the most."

"Oh, Rick," his mom said. She was tearing up.

Andrea started crying again as she bent down and started arranging the three dolls. Baby Softina, Holly Hobbie, and Miss Piggy. "I can't even believe this," she said. "She's going to be . . ." She couldn't finish the sentence.

Rick hurried out to the kitchen and grabbed a knife. He cut open the box and pulled out an Easy-Bake Oven.

"Can I come out now?" Amy yelled.

"Okay if I get her?" Rick asked.

Andrea nodded, wiping her eyes with tissues.

Rick opened his old bedroom door. Amy started to run out, but he stopped her. "Have to close your eyes first."

She obeyed.

"Are they closed?"

"Yes."

"No peeking."

"I'm not."

"Okay then." He stood behind her and walked her to the perfect place to catch the scene.

"Can I open them now?"

"Yes you can," he said.

"Oh my goodness, oh my goodness!" She ran to the

dollhouse first. Then bent down and picked up each doll and gave them a hug. "Are these for me? All these for me?"

"Merry Christmas, Amy," Rick said.

"They're all for you, Amy," Andrea said. "Mr. Rick got them, just for you."

Amy turned around and looked at Rick. She ran and squeezed him as tightly as she could. "Thank you, thank you, thank you," she said. "I've never, ever, ever had a Christmas like this. Not ever."

About ten minutes later, after everyone had regained their composure, Rick asked the three adults to please take a seat. He had a few more presents to pass out. Art sat in his chair, his mom and Andrea on either side of the couch. Amy went over and began to explore the Easy-Bake Oven.

"I'll be right back." He went out to the front seat of the car, grabbed a small bag, and hurried back inside. He pulled out a small wrapped box and handed it to Andrea. Then gave Art a card. "Your present is outside, in the trailer," he said to his mom.

"Who should go first?" Art said.

"Andrea, open yours," Rick said.

She quickly got it open; inside was a card. "Just wanted to fool you a little," he said. "Open it."

She did. Her eyes opened big and wide. "Rick . . . what are these? Disney World? Tickets to Disney World?" She pulled them out of the card.

"What?" Amy yelled and ran over.

"Two sets of tickets," Rick said. Then quickly added, before she might think he was moving too fast, "One for you and one for Amy. She said that's what you'd want, if you could have whatever you wished for."

Amy pulled them out and started flipping through them. "Mom, they're all E-Tickets, every one of them."

Andrea started crying again. She shot up out of her seat and gave Rick another hug. "I don't know what to say."

"You don't have to say anything. Art, now your turn."

Art ripped open his card. His eyes watered right up as he read.

"What is it, Art?" Mom asked.

"Here," was all he could say and handed her the card.

She read it out loud. "Merry Christmas, Art. So glad God spared your life. For Mom's sake and mine. Consider this card a voucher. It's my pledge to go out with you and Father Charlie every Saturday you guys go fishing . . . for the rest of your life." His mom looked up at Rick. "But how can you do this, Rick?"

"It's time for your present," he said. He reached for her hand and helped her off the sofa. "Outside." He led her off the porch, down the sidewalk, and around to the back of the U-Haul trailer.

Everyone followed.

"What is it?" she asked.

Rick took out his keys and unlocked the padlock, then swung the doors open. The trailer was filled with boxes and furniture, crammed to the ceiling. "It's all my stuff. I quit my job in Charlotte. Put my condo up for sale. I'm moving back home for good."

His mom couldn't even speak. She just put her arms around him and squeezed and cried. She stayed there for what felt like five minutes. When she finally got hold of herself, they began walking back toward the house.

"Of course, I'm going to need my old room back, at least for a while," he said. "After New Year's, I'm going to start up my own CPA practice here in Seabreeze. I figure all those rich folks who live along the river and the ocean need somebody they can trust to look after all that money."

"You can stay as long as you want," Art said. "Just as long as you want."

Rick held the door open to let Art, his mom, and Amy

walk through. Andrea held back a few steps and stood on the porch. When he looked into her eyes, he hoped that his mom's present was something she'd like too.

"Rick," she said, holding up her Disney World tickets. "You only bought two sets of these. Amy and I would be willing to wait, if you think you could get hold of a third."

"Oh, believe me," Rick said, "that will *not* be a problem."

51

The Present

Rick sat on the bench across the street from the empty lot where the Book Nook once stood. Today, he decided, would be his last day coming down here. He'd talked with three men in suits yesterday as they walked the property. They said bulldozers would be here tomorrow. Rick didn't think he could bear to see that. Big, noisy machines tearing up this hallowed ground and so many fond memories.

Rick's life had improved dramatically after that Christmas in 1980. Despite the sagging economy, he'd sold his condo in Charlotte within two weeks to the same guy from the firm who'd stolen most of his clients. He got the call confirming the sale the day after he, Andrea, and Amy got back from Disney World in Orlando. It was the best time he'd ever had. Besides the simple escapist pleasures that abound at every turn in the Magic Kingdom, it was also the day Rick knew for certain that Andrea cared for him . . . *that* way.

She didn't hold his hand or say "I love you." They didn't kiss at day's end. But she kept looking at him, and every time he'd notice, she'd smile the sweetest smile. Several times she touched his arm or his shoulder as they turned a corner in line or walked through a doorway. Each time, it was just for a moment. But she'd leave her hand there a moment or two longer than normal. He could still remember the feeling thirty years later. A surge of intense heat. A warmth that lingered. A sensation of joy that remained and increased as the day unfolded.

Andrea had played it safe after that. Got some advice from her pastor that it might be wise not to date Rick for six months, to allow enough time to pass so she could be sure the changes in him were real and for all the right reasons.

Rick didn't mind. She was so worth the wait.

Besides, he got to see her and Amy at the house. They came by often. When the six months were up, Rick picked up a diamond ring and proposed to Andrea on their first date. After a nice dinner and a long walk on the beach.

She said yes . . . without hesitation.

They were married six months later by Father Charlie and after that started attending his church. By then, Rick's CPA practice was doing well enough to support them. During Reagan's second term, the interest rates started falling, and they were able to buy a nice bungalow two streets over from his mom and Art's place.

In the years since, his accounting firm had done extremely well. They bought one of those big fancy houses on the river and kept the bungalow as a rental property. Rick fought off the temptation to buy a big sailboat just so he could cruise up and down the river in the morning, slowly, forcing that old drawbridge to go up and block traffic. The temptation ended five years after he'd bought the riverfront home, when they replaced the bridge with one tall enough for boats to sail right under.

Instead, Rick bought a nice fishing boat. And he'd kept his promise to Art. They went fishing with Father Charlie one or two Saturdays a month for almost twenty years, right up until 1998, when Art passed away. His mom stayed in their little bungalow on Waverly Road. And now they visited her every Saturday evening, brought her dinner and watched a DVD. She moved a little slower, but she was still sharp as a tack.

"Hey, Dad."

Rick looked up. It was Amy, with his two grandkids, Ashley and Charlie, in the backseat. He hadn't even seen her car pull into the parallel parking spot just left of the bench. She yelled through the open car window. "Mom said you'd be down here. I tried calling your cell phone."

"Had it turned off," he said as he stood up and walked over. "Just wanted some time to think."

"Well, I'll leave you alone, just call me when you're done."

"Hey, you guys, how ya doing?" he said, bending down.

"Hi, Poppy!" they yelled back.

"Sorry for interrupting you," Amy said.

"That's all right. I've gotta get back to the office," Rick said.

"Heard about what they're doing across the street. Building a Walgreens or something."

"A CVS."

"That's kind of sad."

"Yeah, it is. So, why were you trying to reach me?"

"Jim and I wanted to know what you thought about having Christmas dinner at our place this year. It's not as big as yours, but it would save Mom a lot of work."

Rick thought about Andrea, how much she loved the holidays. "If she's okay with it."

"I already asked her. She said she'd be fine but that I better ask you."

"Well . . . then let's do it."

"Great. I'll start getting things together and call her later. I'm taking the kids out now for some Christmas shopping around the corner. Did you hear they reopened the Davis Brothers Toy Store?"

"No, I didn't."

"You gotta see it. Brought back all the window displays and everything."

"Really?" Rick wondered if they'd gotten the Lionel trains running up around the ceiling again. "I'll go by there after work."

"I better get going," she said. "Love you."

"Love you too. See ya, kids."

"Bye, Poppy."

Rick had adopted Amy the year after he and Andrea were married. They had joined Art's efforts to reach out to JD. It took almost a year, but they finally coaxed him out of his cardboard box and into a halfway house. They had to promise him that Taylor could live there too. It was nice. Clean, good food. Even had chapel services every Sunday night. Rick would go to his church Sunday mornings and then with his father Sunday nights. Eventually they were able to get JD on the right medication. He seemed to come out of his imaginary world to a degree. Taylor, though, stayed with him till the end. JD died of cirrhosis of the liver in 1994, with Rick and Art by his side.

Rick remembered that he needed to call his son, Jay, born two years after they had gotten married. They were supposed to head out fishing on Saturday. This time with an honored guest. Father Charlie had called, saying he'd be in town for a week. Rick wondered if Charlie would be up for it—he must be about eighty years old now. He gently tried to give Charlie a way out, but Charlie said, "I might be old, Rick, but I'm not dead."

Rick got into his car. A white pickup truck pulled into the lot across the street. Two guys hopped out and pulled a big wooden sign out of the bed. He watched them a few minutes.

One dug holes with a posthole digger. The other stood the sign up and balanced it against the slight wind.

The sign said in big red letters: Coming Soon, CVS!

Life goes on.

In a few months, there'd be a nice building sitting right there and a parking lot full of cars. None of the people going in and out of the new store would have any idea of the miracles and wonders that had taken place on that hallowed ground so many years ago. What had that newspaper article said about it? Rick had kept it in its black frame all these years, mounted on his dresser. He'd read it so many times:

> The Book Nook seems more like an enchanted cottage than a bookstore. A harbor from the cares of life. Some call it a little slice of heaven . . .

And then his favorite part:

> Most, if asked, could not tell you exactly why this is so. But if pressed, they will say it has everything to do with the owners, Art and Leanne Bell. This sweet couple, in equal parts and in their own way, seem to radiate the love of God.

They certainly did, Rick thought.

And because they did, his life had been changed forever.

Author's Note

Remembering Christmas is entirely a work of fiction. Well, sort of.

The little bookstore so central to the story was inspired by an actual Christian bookstore named the Book Nook. The town of Seabreeze is fictitious, but the idea for it came from what I imagined the Daytona Beach area might have looked like had it stayed small; if it had never become "The World's Most Famous Beach" and the birthplace of NASCAR.

Actually, Seabreeze did exist as a little beachside town from 1901 to 1926, when it merged with Daytona Beach to become one city. Seabreeze Boulevard is still one of the main streets in the beachside area, and I graduated from Seabreeze Senior High School, still one of the main public high schools in the Daytona Beach area.

And although everything that happened to Art and Leanne Bell is fictitious, the inspiration for this couple came from a real-life couple who ran that little bookstore in Daytona Beach, out of the basement of an old church. All the other characters in the book, including Rick and Andrea, JD and

Taylor, Father Charlie and all the customers who came in and out of the store, were products of my imagination.

The real-life couple I'm referring to were two of the sweetest, kindest, most caring, generous, and thoughtful people I have ever met. Before we had kids, my wife had the privilege of working for them at the store. It was actually a conversation with her over breakfast, recalling those wonderful days, that gave me the inspiration to write this book.

Acknowledgments

This book is about remembering. I want to take a few moments to remember those who've helped me craft this story and get it to print.

Starting with Cindi, my wonderful wife and greatest friend. She gave me the idea for this book after an enjoyable breakfast together at Cracker Barrel, where we talked about some of the jobs she had in the early years of our marriage. And, as always, she served as "first reader" as I wrote *Remembering Christmas*, offering a number of suggestions and insights along the way.

Then there's my agent, Karen Solem, of Spencerhill Associates. With each year and each book, my respect and esteem for you grows, not just the way you help manage the business side of my writing life, but for your friendship and advice, as well. I also want to thank Andrea Doering, my editor at Revell. I'm so glad to have you as an advocate and advisor. You constantly improve the quality of my stories with your thoughts, ideas, and input. Far from dreading the editorial process, you make it a joy. So glad we have many more books to work on together in the days ahead.

Thanks to Kristin Kornoelje for your keen eye. Thanks to Twila Bennett, Michele Misiak, Karen Wiley, Claudia Marsh, and the whole marketing/publicity team at Revell. You all work so hard to get my books on the shelves and into readers' hands. I can't thank you enough. A special thanks to Cheryl Van Andel and the team responsible for the cover of this book. As soon as I saw it, I wanted to be right there.

Finally, I want to thank Dr. Richard Mabry for answering a number of medical questions. If you find any medical errors in this book, they would be mine, not his. Dr. Mabry is also a fine writer with several medical suspense novels to his credit. You can find out more about them at www.rmabry.com.

Dan Walsh is the award-winning author of *The Unfinished Gift*, *The Homecoming*, and *The Deepest Waters*. A member of American Christian Fiction Writers, Dan served as a pastor for twenty-five years. He lives with his family in the Daytona Beach area, where he's busy researching and writing his next novel.

Meet Dan Walsh at
www.DanWalshBooks.com

Learn more interesting facts, read Dan's blog, and so much more.

Connect with Dan on

f Dan Walsh

t DanWalshAuthor

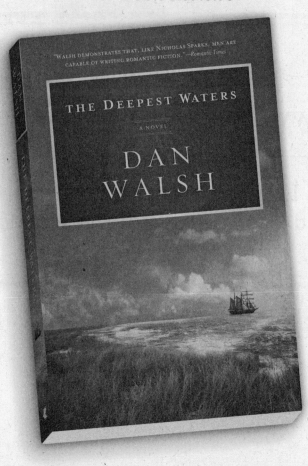

"Make sure you have a tissue nearby, because you are going to need it!"
—TERRI BLACKSTOCK, bestselling author

A YOUNG BOY'S PRAYERS, a shoebox full of love letters, and an old wooden soldier make a memory that will not be forgotten. Can a gift from the past mend a broken heart?

A Reluctant War Hero Returns Home . . . and Encounters a New Chance at Love

A **HEARTWARMING STORY** of tender love
and fresh starts that will capture your heart.